ALTERATIONS TRILOGY

ALTERATIONS
GAME CHANGER
PRIMAL WILL

BOOKS BY JANE SUEN

Children of the Future
Flowers in December

THE ALTERATIONS TRILOGY SERIES
Alterations
Game Changer
Primal Will

SHORT STORIES
Beginnings and Endings: A Selection of Short Stories

ALTERATIONS TRILOGY

ALTERATIONS

GAME CHANGER

PRIMAL WILL

JANE SUEN

ALTERATIONS TRILOGY: Alterations, Game Changer, Primal Will

ALTERATIONS
Copyright © 2017 by Jane Suen

GAME CHANGER: Book 2 of the Alterations Trilogy
Copyright © 2018 by Jane Suen

PRIMAL WILL: Book 3 of the Alterations Trilogy
Copyright © 2018 by Jane Suen

www.janesuen.com

Printed in the United States of America

First Printing: October 2018

Library of Congress Control Number: 2018912116

Paperback ISBN: 978-1-7323873-5-5
Hardback ISBN: 978-1-7323873-6-2
Ebook ISBN: 978-1-7323873-4-8

For my daughter, with love.

Contents

ALTERATIONS

JANE SUEN

Chapter 1
GIGI

GIGI REVVED THE ENGINE OF her old, trusty car. She cranked the window down halfway. Backbone straight, she adjusted her grip on the steering wheel. She focused, bent on reaching her destination, setting her sight on it like a bullseye, having practiced this a million times in her mind—visualizing this moment, every second in slow motion, her mind obsessed with it.

She took one last look in the rearview mirror, fixing her hair and touching up her lipstick. *A girl's gotta look good on this special day.* She had picked the spot. No negotiating or backing out now.

Taking in a deep breath, she held it for a brief second, then let it out with a satisfying *swoosh*.

If her hands were free, she would have been pummeling her chest like Tarzan and making that high-pitched, savage cry. She smiled, picturing Tarzan swinging across the treetops, traveling with exhilarating speed on the canopy highway of the jungle. She allowed herself this final indulgence before pressing on the gas pedal and speeding down the deserted highway, heading straight toward the concrete wall of the curved underpass.

She tightened her grip on the wheel one more time.

At the last moment, an instant before the crash, the wall looming, Gigi's survival instinct kicked in. The tires screeched. Then metal scratched concrete, scraping the front corner and the left side of the car, ripping off the side mirror as she turned the wheel in a desperate attempt to save herself, the car careening one way, then jerking back, before coming to an abrupt stop on the grassy strip on the other side of the highway. The car fizzed as it expelled its final breaths.

Chapter 2
DR. KITE

A WHITE VAN PULLED UP beside the car and two men jumped out, rolling a gurney. They put Gigi, still unconscious, on the stretcher. One man went back to grab her purse, scooping up the contents which spilled in his hurry. He looked around, eyes darting everywhere, keeping a wary watch on the road for vehicles. The other, a taller man, checked her pulse before placing a call on his cell phone.

"We found her." He listened and nodded. "Uh-huh… through the tracking device in her microchip… we're on our way."

The van sped away, leaving no trace. It raced into the city and to a warehouse docking area, disappearing into the dark hollows of the building as the doors swung closed behind it.

The two men wheeled Gigi into a room where a man dressed in medical scrubs was waiting. With his stereoscopic eyepiece, he could be mistaken for a dentist.

"Dr. Kite, she's all yours," the taller man said. He

watched as the doctor carefully examined Gigi, then made a slit in her upper arm, removing a microchip encased in a clear capsule.

"What have I done?" said the doctor as he stared at the chip.

Chapter 3
DR. KITE

GIGI HAD NEVER BEEN SUICIDAL before. Her death wish, propelling her toward an extremely violent end, only came after he implanted this new mind control chip. Did it malfunction, triggering an out-of-character suicide attempt?

Kite looked at Gigi stretched out on the table. *We gave you perfection, how could you not want that? No disease, no malfunctioning organs, every cell optimized and in perfect working order.*

And she would never have to worry as long as the microchip was inside her. She was a lucky one. Every healthy cell programmed to copy and regenerate on a timetable, every sick cell targeted to die. It was his masterpiece.

He conducted hundreds of scientific experiments, working tirelessly until he successfully developed his products. Gigi had been implanted with one of his three earlier prototypes. That original microchip needed an enhancement, long overdue, so they called her in last week to implant a new second-generation, upgraded model with mind control and a tracking device.

If only, this time, they *could* control the mind. The body they could now fix—not just for cosmetic reasons, but to cure people who were ill like Gigi, destroying the defective cells and replacing them with healthy ones. Once he perfected this microchip, he would have riches beyond imagination. How many people? Millions, no *billions*. Why, he'd even offer different grades of this microchip to make it more affordable. He could almost hear the people clamoring for it.

He touched Gigi's face. She had been cleaned up, every trace of the near-crash removed. He sighed. The upgraded mind control chip he'd implanted—he had been so close to the ultimate success. But he wasn't there yet. What went wrong today? Had it tried to make Gigi do something against her nature? Did she suppress or override its mind control? Was the chip ineffective or defective? With a shrug, he turned, walked across the room to retrieve Gigi's original chip from storage, then re-implanted it in her arm.

The taller man wheeled Gigi down the hall and into a vast room filled with drawers. He slid her into an empty cabinet and rolled it shut. On the keypad next to it, he selected the "Regenerate" button.

Chapter 4
LILLY

THEY LET GIGI SLEEP. AND sleep well she did that night, undisturbed in the hard cocoon of her drawer, kept warm and quiet, accompanied by the soft hum of the equipment. Nothing was left to chance that might stand in the way of optimal recovery for Dr. Kite's patients. Especially Gigi. Tonight was a tough night, with Kite worrying about Gigi again. Her actions and movements were becoming more erratic since he implanted the new upgrade a few days ago. She wasn't as careful about making good choices, getting out of control. Something was going wrong with the new chip, so he'd secretly rescued her and healed her from the accident, because he didn't want her to know.

When he was in medical school, he was a bright-eyed idealist. He wanted to be the next great healer. He wasn't the most brilliant scientist in the world, but he had other talents—an astute mind that seized upon a chance discovery, and the drive and persistence to succeed. Before that, he had an interest in electrical engineering. After earning a bachelor's degree in that field, Kite worked as a test engineer in the wireless microchip and biomedical industries. His combined interest led him to this project. It took him twenty-two years to do it, to make changes, refine, improve, and test this new chip technology. *Now,* he thought, *it's close to the finish line.*

As he pulled out of the warehouse, Kite nodded to the guys. He could hear his mother's refined voice saying, "Be nice to everyone." Driving in the quiet of the evening relaxed him. What happened to Gigi shook him up. Needing time to think, unwind, and relieve some of the tension his body still carried from the day, he headed into the parking lot of Duggers—his favorite restaurant where he felt like, and was treated like, royalty.

"Good evening, doctor," said the hostess, flashing him a warm smile she reserved for special customers.

"Good to see you, Sally," said Kite. Leaning closer he murmured, "I, um… I've been busy and don't have a reservation for tonight. Perhaps you could get me a seat?"

"Your usual place?"

"Yes, please."

Sally picked up a menu and led the way to his table. She thought it was empty, but as she approached, it was clear a woman was sitting there, alone. Sally turned around, facing Kite. "Oh, I'm sorry…"

Kite glanced at the woman, fighting his disappointment. "That's all right. You can seat me at the other table."

Sally looked relieved but sought his assurance. "You're sure that's all right? I've never seen you at another table. This is your lucky table, as you always say," she gushed, a nervous squeak in her voice.

"Tonight is this lady's lucky night," Kite said with a gracious wave.

The woman at the table watched him. A trace of a smile flickered across her face.

He gave her the briefest nod, holding her glance for a moment longer.

"Well in that case, let me share my luck," the lady said. "Would you like to join me?"

Her invitation caught him by surprise. He was still ruffled, but his well-bred exterior betrayed no such thing. He gave a slight bow in thanks before extending his hand. "Dr. Kite, at your service."

"I'm Lilly Cooper." They shook hands.

"Ms. or Mrs., may I ask?" Kite said as he pulled back the chair to sit across from her.

"The former Mrs. Cooper. Perhaps you know my ex-husband, Frank Cooper?"

"I'm afraid not."

"He introduced me to this place. We used to come here often. It was popular in the day. It's farther now, since I've moved, but I still come here on occasion." She paused. "But Frank stopped coming," she added.

"I hope I'm not disturbing you."

"Oh no, not at all. I've had my peace and quiet while I enjoyed my meal. This is perfect timing—I've just ordered coffee and dessert."

"I don't believe I've seen you here," said Kite as he leaned forward and spoke with friendliness in his naturally deep voice, determined to have a good evening. "Today's *my* lucky day. I appreciate your generosity in sharing your table with me."

"I believe in luck, Dr. Kite," cooed Lilly. "I need all the luck I can get."

Chapter 5
GIGI

GIGI WOKE UP WITH A slight headache. It was dark. She tried to remember where she was and what she was doing. She touched her face. Lying in the darkness, she reached out with her fingers to explore her surroundings. She pushed against a hard surface, feeling its smoothness. She panicked, thinking she was in a coffin. This can't be happening! *Calm down*, she chided herself.

Last night, Gigi had tossed and turned. Her body craved rest, but her mind stayed wired up, even knowing she was safe at home, in her own bedroom, on her bed. Her mind was running, trying to get away, fighting to stay awake, dreading the terrifying nightmare that had presented itself for a few nights in a row since she got the upgraded microchip. But, despite her efforts, she eventually fell into an uneasy rest. Something wasn't right.

She went over the events now, trying to recall, to bring back a memory. As hard as she tried, she couldn't remember. That irked her. Wanting to retrieve a piece of her memory which may be the key to unlocking the mystery of what happened, she closed her eyes to concentrate. She was in her car, checking herself in the rearview mirror. Sometime after that it became fuzzier. It had to be important. Racking her brain to think hurt.

She checked the rest of her body, reaching as far she could. She was all there, no missing parts or limbs. She wiggled her toes and moved her legs and arms. To be sure, she pinched herself. *Ouch.* Sure felt that.

Bits and pieces flashed in front of her eyes—the looming concrete wall, the interior of her car, her foot slamming on the brake, the loud screeching, and then nothing more. Well, something must have happened, but she didn't die. Was she in a car accident? A fender bender? But she wasn't in pain, and she wasn't hurting. No broken bones. *Now c'mon Gigi, think. Try and remember as much as you can.* She vaguely recalled someone looking at her, soft murmurs, and being transported in a vehicle.

So what was this place? There didn't seem to be a latch of any kind on the inside she could push or pull. She could hear something whirling. Gigi strained, hoping to gain a clue of her whereabouts. Relief flooded her as she realized she didn't die in fiery flames or an injury so bad that inflicted broken bones, crushed vital organs, or left her paralyzed. What had she been doing? She was determined to find the answers.

As Gigi pondered what to do next, she heard a spraying sound and felt a cooling mist. In a panic, she pushed hard, trying to get out, fearful of being gassed to death. There was nowhere to escape. Gigi put her hand over her mouth, pinched her nose, and held her breath. But that didn't work. The mist began filling the space, covering her, and she finally succumbed to sleep, a deep slumber.

Her body regenerated, cell by cell.

Chapter 6
DR. KITE

WHEN MORNING CAME, KITE WAS up early, a habit he had acquired during his early years in medical school when he worked long days and was on call through the night. Sleeping late was a luxury he only allowed himself on rare occasions, even to this day. He had received a text during the night and approved the administration of a mist to help Gigi sleep as her body regenerated overnight. It was in her best interest. Anxious to see her, he rushed back at the break of dawn.

Kite smiled. Today was turning out better than he ever imagined. As soon as he arrived, he checked on Gigi. If they hadn't gotten to her within minutes, she may have died from her injuries. She was lucky to be alive and under his watchful eye. The microchip he'd inserted last night, her original one, appeared to work fine. Satisfied with her quick recovery through the night, he approved her release. He made final preparations, calculating how much time remained before she'd wake up. Then he summoned the two men who had brought her in yesterday.

They worked efficiently, putting Gigi back in the white van along with her purse and driving to a hotel parking deck nearby. They half-dragged her into the elevator and hit the button for the lobby floor. As soon as the elevator doors opened, they propped an almost-awake Gigi between their arms and carried her to a chair out of sight of the security cameras. In the few minutes remaining before she woke up, they made her comfortable while standing in front of her, blocking any inquisitive glances. The timing was perfect, the crowd of guests checking out keeping the hotel staff busy. The taller man made a call to Kite.

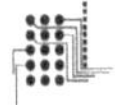

The doctor was in fabulous spirits. He called himself a doctor, but if anybody checked, they wouldn't be able to find his medical degree or license. In truth, Kite didn't even finish medical school. He dropped out midway through his fourth year. In his mind, he was still a doctor, and thought he had every right to call himself one. Nobody had ever questioned him, or his credentials. In his white coat, he exuded authority and confidence.

He passed by the monitor room. All the lights were green, the rows of screens lit up, one for each of the sleeping bodies in the cabinets, the new people brought in each night. The next morning, they'd be rotated out, released back to the world once he'd examined them. These were people they found passed out on sidewalks, lost travelers—anyone not likely to be missed for a few hours.

They had a fake taxicab that trawled the city at night, picking up rides. But as a rule, only single passengers. Most of the time, the riders were too drunk or high to be aware of what was happening. They could barely talk or walk. The overnight stay was just a precaution, in case of an adverse reaction to the microchip. If that occurred, then Kite would remove it. The person was released, and nobody was any the wiser.

Chapter 7
GIGI

When Gigi didn't come home, Rex was up all night, worried. It was so unlike her not to call if she'd be late. He drove to her favorite spots and scouted around. He looked for her car in all the places he could think of. His calls went straight to voice mail. She never picked up or called back. He grew more frantic as the night faded and the first light announced a new day. By then, Rex was so tired he nodded off while he was driving. Several times he startled himself, jerking awake before almost running into another car. It was pointless to keep going. Surely she'd be home by now, he thought, while driving back to the apartment.

Seeing no signs of her dashed his hopes. He headed inside to catch a quick nap, knowing he wouldn't last through the day otherwise. Rex placed another call to her cell phone and left a frantic, semi-coherent message before crashing on the living room sofa, falling into a deep sleep.

The alarm on his cell phone startled him. He had set the timer to wake him up at 9:30 a.m. Yawning loudly and stretching, he turned it off and got up to make a pot of coffee. While it was brewing, he took a quick shower. Four hours wasn't enough sleep, but the shower refreshed him.

Rex poured a large cup of coffee and sat down to make a list of all the places he had checked already. He tried hard to think of where else Gigi might have gone. It troubled him. This was so unlike her. He placed a call to the office to let them know he wasn't coming in. He liked having the flexibility of being a part-time reporter. As long as he turned his assignments in on time, they left him alone.

Organized and methodical, he crafted a plan including people to call—her friends, family, their mutual acquaintances, anyone who might know where she could be. He called her cell phone again, counting the rings before he left her another message. "Hey, this is Rex, call me *please*. I'm worried. Where are you?"

He went to the kitchen and refilled his cup. Hearing his cell phone jingle with her special ring tone, he rushed back to grab it, spilling hot coffee on his jeans.

"Hello…"

"Oh, Rex…"

"Gigi? Gigi! Where are you?"

"Rex, please come and get me."

"Where? What happened?"

"I… I need your help," she pleaded. "Please hurry. I'm at Hotel Seven."

"On my way," said Rex as he ran out the door, car key in his hands. "I'll be there in about fifteen minutes."

"Okay, I'm inside the lobby." Her phone chirped. "I

need to charge my phone. My battery's going to die at any minute. Got to go."

Rex drove as fast as he dared, mouthing a silent prayer of thanks for the light traffic and hoping he wouldn't get a ticket. He could tell that Gigi wasn't her usual self; she sounded different, maybe even a little scared. That was weird. Rex's impatience matched his speed, his imagination running wild. Where had she been? What happened to her?

Relief was replacing the worry that caused so much angst the night before. His whirling emotions also brought out his feelings for Gigi, and Rex realized they ran deeper than he thought. Well, they were roommates and got along fine. No, cross that out, they were *more* than just roommates. They were best friends. Countless times they helped each other out, and laughed and cried together over the years. They had both dated other people off and on, and in between joked about their nonexistent sex life after their relationships fell through. She'd cried on his shoulder and confided in him. He sought her opinion when he had girlfriend troubles. They had been through so much over the years, staying together as friends while boyfriends or girlfriends came and went. So he knew her pretty well, and he felt sure she knew him.

Rex pulled up in front of Hotel Seven just in time. He didn't see her outside, so he parked and ran into the building to find her. Heart pounding, he panicked when he didn't see her right away. As he scanned the lobby, he spotted her— sitting in a far corner next to the electric outlet she was using to charge her phone.

She jumped up when he rushed across. "You're here!" she shouted, a smile replacing the worried look on her face.

He reached out and wrapped his arms around her, slowly swaying from side to side while hugging her, not willing to let go just yet.

"Gigi, are you all right?" he finally said, pulling back to inspect her.

Gigi nodded. She looked disheveled, her clothes crumpled. She raised her hand, flipping back her hair. "I'm fine. Just a little sore, that's all."

He held her again, rubbing her back gently. "Look, we need to go now. I've got my car parked in front."

She yanked her charger from the wall socket and grabbed her purse. "I could do with a shower and a change of clothing."

On the way out, he maintained protective contact, guiding her by the elbow toward his car. "Maybe I should take you to the hospital, get you checked out first?"

She glanced at him, mumbling, "I don't know… I think I'm okay." She patted her arms, chest, and legs. "I'm all here and in one piece." She added, "I promise I'll let you know if I need to see a doctor."

Rex didn't want to make a fuss. Not here. Not now. They got into his car and he sped straight home.

While Gigi jumped in the shower and freshened up, Rex made breakfast and brewed a fresh pot of coffee. He searched in the refrigerator and found a carton of orange juice, knowing how she liked a little glass of OJ with her breakfast. By the time Gigi finished and got changed, breakfast was on the table.

"Thank you," squealed Gigi as she hugged Rex again. "It smells so good."

Rex was hungry too, he realized, as his own stomach growled. They sat down and ate, not bothering to talk while they gobbled down the eggs and hash potatoes. Satisfied, Rex pushed his plate out of the way and leaned back in his chair.

"So, tell me what happened," he said.

"I don't know how much I remember. It was so odd." Gigi hesitated, searching for the right words. "I think I did something horrible."

Rex waited, knowing she would tell him eventually and it would all come out, piece by piece. That's how they shared and communicated with each other. He let her have as much time as she needed. "I worried about you all night," said Rex. "I kept calling you."

Gigi swallowed, then continued. "I tried to ram my car into a wall. Swerved at the last instant averting a full impact."

"You did… what?"

"I'm sorry, I remember little of what happened after that." She frowned. "I was out… I thought I was, or maybe I dreamt I was laying in a coffin or container." She stared into space trying to recall. "I mean, it was fuzzy. If I'd heard your phone ring, I would have answered." Taking another sip of coffee, Gigi repeated, "You know I would have answered. Maybe I passed out or something like that, and I didn't hear it? That would be a plausible explanation."

"Let's assume that you were unconscious, or out of it after the accident. That may explain why you couldn't remember or didn't hear the phone ring," said Rex. "So what happened when you did wake up? You called me, right?"

"I think so. I heard my phone ring and it woke me up. I must have passed out on the chair in the hotel lobby. When I saw your number on the screen, I called you right back."

"Gosh, does that mean you were out for a long time?"

"Yeah, I suppose."

"So is your car at the hotel?"

"I don't know where my car is."

"Well we should go back over there and look around for it."

Rex drove straight to the hotel parking deck, grabbing a ticket before entering. Crawling at a snail's pace, they looked and checked every vehicle. As they rounded the curve to the exit booth, it became clear that Gigi's car wasn't there.

Finally, Rex suggested widening the search, circling the hotel, combing every side street. This took longer than they thought. They finished by noon, no closer to finding the car than they were in the morning.

Chapter 8

ELLEN

ELLEN WAS LATE WHEN SHE rushed with her new dress and accessories out of the boutique. She was still pissed at the smooth-talking saleslady encouraging her to try on everything, making suggestions if something didn't work out. Drove her nuts! She wanted to scream and yell, "Don't be so pushy!" She knew the kind. No matter how she looked in the dress, the woman always said, "Ooh, I love this one, it looks great on you." *Ugh.*

Ellen wasn't fooled, knowing full well how she looked. She'd endured cruel taunts for most of her life about her weight, but they got uglier as she got older. Mean, hurtful remarks like, "get that through your fat skull," "fat ass bitch," "you're better off stepping in front of a bus." The bullies from the playground grew up, but they never changed inside.

She'd had to escape from the saleswoman. Worn out and exasperated, Ellen made a quick selection—a stylish dress catching her attention, but one she knew was too small—

just to get rid of the woman. It wasn't an easy way out—an expensive choice, definitely hard on her pocketbook.

The rush-hour traffic was horrendous. Cars inched along, creeping and crawling. Ellen had no patience, tapping her fingers on the wheel as she looked around, waiting for the light to change. To her left was another shopping strip. A sign caught her eye. Eve's Alterations. On impulse, she flicked her turn signal, waving to the man driving his truck toward her in the opposite lane to catch his attention. She flashed her cutest smile. He smiled back and stopped, letting her make the turn.

Men liked Ellen if all they could see was her pretty face.

Ellen parked, grabbing the bag with her new dress. Clutching the undersized garment, she had to admit how much she liked it despite it being the wrong size, so much so that she'd fantasized wearing it and showing off at her cousin's wedding. Ever since she got the invitation in the mail, she was obsessed with the thought of going back home looking good, *damn good*. The hometown girl is not looking frumpy. She'd show up at the wedding and dazzle everyone. Okay, that was just wishful thinking. She reluctantly dropped the dress back in the shopping bag. Maybe, if this seamstress was worth her salt, she could look stunning.

A bell announced her entrance as Ellen opened the door.

"Hello. Anyone here?" said Ellen, peering inside. It was a plain room with a counter, a cash register, and a curtained changing room.

"Wait a minute, be out soon," a female voice called from the back.

"Okay," Ellen shouted. Waiting, she glanced around and

saw two displays on the wall—the business license and another cheap frame with a mounted dollar bill. It was considered good luck to save the first dollar bill earned, rather than spend it. No other decorations graced the walls. It was what she expected. Alterations was what she came here for, not some fancy interior decorating.

The curtain was pulled aside, and a diminutive, dark-haired woman appeared.

"Hello," she said with a smile. "You come here."

"Hi, I'm Ellen. You are Eve?"

"Eve."

Ellen held up her new dress, flaunting it. The vivid deep blue, the V-neck, the hand-beaded lace bodice, and the three-quarter length sleeves were dazzling.

The seamstress gestured Ellen closer, then made a circle with her finger. "Turn around please." She held up the dress to Ellen's back, measuring with her well-trained eyes. It didn't take her more than a second to realize the dress was about two to three sizes smaller. She stared at Ellen and said, "You *like* this dress?"

"Oh *yes*, very much," Ellen said, nodding emphatically. "I'm planning to wear it to a wedding." Ellen had lost thirty-five pounds already, coming down three dress sizes. But still at one fifty-five, she had a ways to go. Her goal of losing another thirty pounds before the wedding now appeared hopeless, along with fitting into this gorgeous size six dress.

The seamstress handed the dress back to Ellen. "Okay, I know what you need." She opened a drawer behind the counter, picking up a brochure to show Ellen.

"What's this?" Ellen asked.

"This is for a special lady like you," Eve said.

"Tell me what it is."

"You look…" Eve said, handing her the brochure.

Curious, Ellen's eyes scanned the contents.

"This brochure, it's not about the sewing alterations," said Ellen. "It says, 'Instant body slimming for the look you desire.'" Her eyes skimmed to the price column, but all it said was MARKET PRICE. It looked like a Chinese restaurant menu. "How much is the market price?"

"Which one you want? See here," said Eve as she pointed to the three choices. "Option A, Size 6, in the middle Option B, Size 8, and on the right Option C, Size 10. You pick."

"I don't understand. I thought 'alterations' is for the dress—or a blouse, pants, suit…" She paused.

"No alteration dress, alteration your body to fit dress." Eve pulled out a tablet. "Let me show you." She scrolled through a series of photos labeled "Before" and "After"— each having a silhouette of a body next to the dress. The only thing that changed from "Before" to "After" was the size of the person.

Ellen felt a chill run up her back as she realized what Eve was showing her. The photos showed the size of the *person* had been altered—not the dress.

"How do you get smaller to fit into the dress?" Ellen was interested, although perplexed at the same time.

Eve said, "No operation." She scrolled to the page with the three options. "You pick one."

Curious to see where this was going, Ellen played along, entering the size of her new dress. Option A appeared with the text, "Are you sure you want Option A, Size 6?"

Ellen touched the YES button. Then, the page displayed an appointment time for that evening with an address.

Eve went to the back room and returned with a printed sheet for Ellen. "All done."

"Do I pay you now?"

"No pay me. When you go to appointment."

Ellen looked at the slip. The date and time was tonight at 8:00 p.m. That left just enough time to get a quick bite at the drive-through. She grabbed her dress, hurrying out.

Chapter 9

ELLEN

Ellen GOT TO THE APPOINTMENT location early. Relaxing in her car seat, she thought about the whole day—a whirlwind, running from meeting to meeting, eating on the run, fighting the traffic. Closing her eyes, she went over what Eve said. Ellen could tell that Eve, the seamstress, either didn't know the answers or wasn't able to explain to her satisfaction what the options entailed. She would ask her questions and find out tonight.

The location on the sheet Eve gave her was at the corner of two streets. It didn't have an exact street number or name of the business. Ellen scanned the building in sight. It was strange. Absorbed in studying the map on her cell phone, she didn't see or hear the man until he tapped on her car window, startling her.

"Are you Ellen?"

"Who… are you? How did you know?"

"You can get out of your car and follow me," he said, not bothering to answer her questions.

"I'm here for my appointment, but I don't know where to go."

"Just follow me. I'm here to take you there."

She grabbed the dress and her appointment slip. Leaving her car parked by the side of the street, she locked it and followed the man to the nondescript office building at the corner.

He pointed inside, leaving as she entered the lobby. On the wall before the elevators, Ellen saw the directory of businesses. Reading through the names, she ruled out, by a process of elimination, businesses that obviously didn't fit. That narrowed it down to two possibilities.

She typed both of those office numbers in her cell phone notes and rode the elevator to the first one on the second floor. Ellen knocked on the office door and waited. No one came to the door or answered. She knocked again. Nothing. So she went back in the elevator and pushed the fourth floor button. She found Room 408 at the end of the hallway. At first knock, a young man opened the door and welcomed her. "Hello."

"Hi, I'm Ellen. My appointment is at 8:00 p.m."

"Yes, we're expecting you. I'm Daman. Please come in and have a seat in this room. The doctor will be with you in a minute."

Ellen walked in, surprised at the pleasant surroundings. Fresh white paint covered the walls. Together with the minimalist white furniture and the stylish tiny reception desk, it conveyed a crisp, clean, no-nonsense atmosphere.

"Can you tell me about the procedure?"

"The doctor will explain it to you."

"It's not an operation is it?" she asked with concern, letting him know she was not up to something like that. "I hate surgeries; they scare me."

He reassured her, speaking in a cheerful way. "No ma'am, we don't do that here. You'll be out of here soon." He paused and added, "And looking great."

"Oh," she said as the doctor stepped into the room to greet her.

"Good evening, you must be Ellen. I'm Dr. Kite."

She extended her hand. "Hi, yes, I'm Ellen Fulbright. Nice to meet you, Doctor."

"Come with me. We'll sit down and talk first." She followed him down the hall to his office, and he waved for her to sit. "I know you have questions. Now, what would you like to know?"

Ellen pursed her lips. "I selected Option A on the menu for Size 6 dress." She pulled out her dress for him to see, shaking it for emphasis. "How do you get me to fit into this dress?"

He was ready for her. "You selected Option A. When you walk out of here tonight, you'll be wearing that dress."

"But how is that possible? I *don't* want anyone to operate on me."

"There's no surgery. I assure you. It will be a gentle and quick, and you will not feel any pain." He paused, reaching on his desk for a pen—well, something that looked like a pen. "See this?"

She nodded, wondering why he was holding it.

"Inside is a mini-syringe. Injection is quick and painless—just a small pinch, hardly more than a mosquito bite." Kite touched the pen on his arm to show her.

"What are you injecting?"

"I will insert a tiny microchip inside your body. It will adjust your metabolism to what you eat."

"How does your chip work?"

"It works on a cellular level, regulating the mitochondria. Your chip increases the rate of fat metabolism."

"You mean I can still eat whatever I want, and how much I want?"

"Not exactly. It will have to work harder if you eat more. So I suggest eating smaller portions at more frequent intervals. Can you do that?"

"I've been on a diet and lost thirty-five pounds, cutting out a lot of carbs and eating less."

"So you want to lose more weight?"

"Well I need help now. I've been struggling to get the last thirty pounds off and *nothing* I do seems to make a difference."

"We'll give a boost to blast the fat cells tonight that'll take about twenty minutes. That will drop you down to the size you selected immediately. Then the procedure to inject the microchip takes a few seconds. But remember, to maintain your size six, you must also change your eating habits."

"What happens if I don't… if I forget?"

"We've programmed a reminder, adjusted to the level of overconsumption and pain threshold."

"Pain? What kind of pain?" Ellen asked, shifting in her seat.

"It's a mild reminder at first, like a tiny prick." He

quickly added, "But if it's too much, we can tweak it."

"I… I'm not sure I like that." She hesitated.

"The pain reminder?"

"Yeah."

"Hmm," he said, sighing. "On second thought, no—instead I'm going to use the new second-generation, upgraded chip I just got. It has a mind control element to ensure you'll change your behavior."

"Mind control?"

"Yes, the new chips have this, an enhancement over the older chip that uses pain to control behavior."

"So, uh, I won't get a pain reminder?

"Right. I just received this new shipment. There's one with the blue label for overweight clients. You'll get that one."

"That sounds too good to be true."

"It's the best I can offer you."

"Will I look different tonight after this procedure?"

"You'll be thinner, just like in the photos you've seen. And you'll fit into your size six dress."

"How safe is this new procedure?"

"It's safe. We've had no problems. You can think about it and call me later if you have more questions."

She stared at him intently. "It really works *and* it's safe?"

"Yes." He pushed back his chair to stand. "Do you want to think it over, or shall we do it tonight?"

"One more question. If I change my mind, can you remove this chip?"

"At any time, if you request it. And I'll give you this one-time offer of a free trial period."

"Okay, then I'm ready," said Ellen, smiling as she stood up.

Ellen followed Kite down the hall to another white room lit with soft lights. A white pod was in the middle of the room. A table stood next to it with a tray on top. A pen lay on the tray next to a strip of alcohol pads and gauze.

"Please lie down in the pod. You can take your clothes off and leave your underwear on, then drape this sheet over yourself. I'll give you a few minutes and come back."

After he left, Ellen inspected the pod. It looked elegantly designed, a white, clamshell-like structure that appeared translucent. Ellen put her dress over the chair and took off her clothes down to her lace bra and panties before climbing a white two-step stool into the pod. She smoothed the cloth over her, scooping her long hair to one side and closing her eyes. She sensed his presence a moment before he spoke.

"Ellen, I want you to relax and keep your eyes closed. Visualize your new look, your new size. I will close the lid of the pod, but you will still be able to hear me."

He kept talking for a few minutes in a soothing voice. She drifted in and out of wakefulness, waiting for the procedure and thinking, *when will this happen?* She tried to calm her unease and assure herself that this wasn't an operation. Ellen finally relaxed and fell asleep. At some point, the clamshell opened and she thought she felt a slight pinch on her arm.

"You may get up whenever you are ready."

Ellen opened her eyes. The doctor was gone. *What? Is it done already?*

She looked around, then touched herself with the tips of her fingers—exploring. She slowly sat up, and then swung her leg out to climb out of the clamshell, placing her foot on the step stool first.

Someone had taken her dress and hung it on a hanger. Slipping the dress over her head, Ellen felt it glide over her body. She knew. *Without a doubt.*

The doctor and Daman greeted her when she rushed to the door and opened it. The looks on their faces said it all, without a single word exchanged. Ellen was ecstatic. She twirled around, showing off how she looked from every angle, adding a dance step or two as a bonus.

The younger guy grinned from ear to ear. Adjusting the standing mirror to provide a better view, he said, "Here, have a look."

Chapter 10

GIGI

REX'S FIRST IDEA SHOULD HAVE been to call the wreckers or impound lots. Without wasting more time, they went back home. While he searched on the Internet, Gigi went to lie down. He checked in on Gigi as she slept. He didn't disturb her; letting her sleep was the best thing for her right now. He left a note, tacking the yellow sticky on her night table where she would be sure to see it when she woke up. The note told her where he would be—at the office—and to call him when she awoke.

Rex got out his keys and left. It bugged him he couldn't do more than he did. She had been through a lot. Yet, he wondered if there was more that she hadn't yet shared with him. Sometimes she held back, not because she wasn't upfront with him, but because she didn't want him to worry about her. What good would that do? One of them had to be the sane one at all times. He respected that. She was right about most things. It wasn't as if he would stop worrying, but he knew talking helped to take a load off her mind. He was that person, that confidant, that best friend.

Rex stepped off the elevator and walked through the press offices to his cubicle. He had another, ulterior motive for coming in today. Scrolling through his contact list, he found his friend Steve, who was a consultant and sometimes a private investigator after his retirement from the force. He dialed his number.

"Hi buddy, Rex."

"Oh, hey," said Steve, genuinely glad to hear from him. "How've you been?"

"Doing good. And you?"

"Can't say I have any complaints." He paused. "How's Gigi?"

Rex gave Steve a rundown of what had happened to Gigi. He wanted Steve's perspective. Maybe he was missing something. Not willing to leave it at that, he told Steve everything. Steve was superb at what he did. And if anyone could help, he could.

"I'm just in a rut, Steve," confessed Rex, running his fingers through his hair. "Something doesn't seem right, and Gigi can't remember what happened. It's like someone or something wiped her memory clean for those hours."

"I know you're worried, Rex. Let me see what I can find out."

Rex could hear Steve clicking on the computer while they talked.

"Thanks, Steve. I'm grateful for anything you can do to help."

"I'm looking at reports of cars or accidents. Do you have the vehicle information and the tag number of Gigi's car?"

"Yes, it's an old car." Rex read out the tag number and gave Steve the year, make, model, and color. He could hear more clicking.

"Ah… here," said Steve. "I found a report of an abandoned car near the Highway 15 underpass. The description matches Gigi's car." He continued after a brief pause. "You'd better get there fast. They'll be taking her car to impound."

"I'll go get Gigi. Thanks, man."

Chapter 11

ELLEN

Ellen stood naked in front of the floor-length mirror in her bedroom. Her eyes scrutinized every part of her body from her head to her toes. She turned around, craning her neck over her shoulder. She sauntered back and forth in front of the mirror, admiring her perfect body—the proportionate curves, perky round breasts, smooth flat stomach, long tapering legs, and firm butt. She looked better than she ever had. *Way* better. She smiled as she strutted confidently, head held high.

Her cousin's upcoming wedding increased the pressure on her. Ellen had struggled with her weight for years and tried just about every diet and exercise program. Her tummy area was the worst. She hadn't been able to get rid of the fat there. Her hips, butt, and outer thighs padded fat faster than she could get rid of it.

Every choice of clothing was calculated to camouflage her problems. The dress sizes increased with the years. It became hopeless, affecting other aspects of her life. It wasn't just her weight that dragged down her confidence, but also the depressing thought of the not-too-distant future, in a few years, when she would turn forty.

She was tired of it all. She didn't know what to do anymore. Nothing she did ever worked for long. Sure, she had lost weight with some diets, but gained it all back eventually. She got to the point where she was disgusted whenever she looked in the mirror—each time she'd spent more money and chased after a new fad diet.

Ellen had reached the point of desperation when she met Kite. She had to do something—something that she couldn't achieve herself, and it had to be something that worked fast, in time for the wedding. Kite promised that and delivered—he got rid of that fat immediately and gave Ellen a new body—a total body transformation. She absolutely loved it.

She left the doctor's office elated. He told her it was time phased. This was a trial run at no cost. If she wanted to keep going, she would need to pay. It was expensive, but in the long run, cheaper than an operation. Kite gave her a stern reminder about the expiration date and time, which turned out to be six days after the Saturday wedding at 8:30 p.m. If she didn't pay by then, the time would expire on the microchip. The doctor emphasized the importance of the deadline. If she waited past the deadline, it would be too late, and the door on that offer would shut forever.

Chapter 12
GIGI

"GIGI," WHISPERED REX AS HE shook her shoulders gently. "Wake up, they found your car." He waited, then shook her again, more firmly this time. He spoke with more urgency. "Get up now."

She stirred and moved her body ever so slightly. "What?" she mumbled.

"Gigi, they found your car. Get up. We need to go *now*."

Her eyes popped open. "My car? Where is my car?"

"It's near the Highway 15 underpass."

Gigi jumped out of bed, awake now. She yelled, "Give me a minute, I'll be right out."

"I'll be waiting in the car," said Rex, rushing out the door.

Rex drove as fast as he dared to the Highway 15 underpass. He knew the place, having passed through there many times. As they approached, it was evident the guy from the wrecker service was already there getting ready to tow her car.

"*Wait*, please wait a minute," shouted Rex as he and Gigi ran toward him.

The guy looked up as he hopped on the bed of the truck, checking the tow straps and fiddling with the tow chains. "Is that your car?"

"Yes. We'd like to take a quick look. Can you please wait?" pleaded Rex, the urgency in his voice matching his expression.

"You got about a minute until I get this chain untangled."

They approached the car, which was parked at an angle on the grassy strip area next to the highway. From the looks of the tire marks and tracks on the grass, the car had swerved at the last minute to avoid running into the concrete wall, so the force of the hit was not full frontal, but it had sheared off the side rearview mirror and damaged the corner and the side of the car where it scraped the underpass wall. A few pieces of paper lay scattered on the grass on the driver side, where they had blown out of the half rolled-down window. It was very fortunate that Gigi didn't run straight into the wall. The car could have exploded in flames, engulfing and destroying the vehicle with her inside.

"Do you think it's totaled?" blurted Rex, even though he knew the answer.

The wrecker guy gave a sympathetic nod, then finished hooking up the chains and pulling the car onto his flatbed. Before he left, he gave Rex a card. "Call this number."

"Thanks, man."

Rex looked over at Gigi. She had been silent as she surveyed the accident scene. He hoped she wasn't traumatized. Survivor shock, PTSD, emotional trauma—those could stay with you long afterwards. He remembered his first car, a tiny little Volks. Oh, how he enjoyed driving that thing until someone rear-ended him one day. *Pow!* The moment of impact, his body jerking, his head thrown back and forth. He had been shaken and couldn't stop trembling. That memory still lingered on.

This incident happened in an odd place. What was Gigi doing there? Why did she pick this location? The underpass was off the beaten path and not in a well-traveled territory.

Rex watched the tow truck pull away and waited until the dust settled before approaching Gigi, who was still sitting on the grass. He scooted next to her. They sat for a while, staring in silence at the empty spot where her car had been. Finally, he leaned forward to whisper in her ear. "You feeling okay?"

"Yeah, but not about the accident. I mean, it *was* an accident, right? It had to be." She looked confused, searching for answers. "I don't remember what I was doing here or why I drove this way. I don't know why I'd be running into the wall or why I didn't." She gestured wildly, pointing to the concrete barrier, then shuddered.

"Just calm down. Do you remember anything? Anything at all? Try to go back over the steps if you can."

"I tried… can't…" She sighed.

"Were you swerving to avoid hitting someone? A dog or a critter… like a squirrel?"

"I don't remember… why would I ram it?"

"Well, you're lucky you didn't. Else I wouldn't be sitting here talking to you."

Gigi twisted her face, feeling the tears welling up. Then she released her pent-up emotions, holding nothing back. He wrapped his arms around her, comforting her, feeling the weight of her head resting on his shoulder as she cried, her tears soaking the cotton of his shirt.

Chapter 13
DR. KITE

KITE PICKED UP THE PHONE. "Okay, bring her here. I'll be ready." He had been waiting for this call. When it finally happened, he was pleased. Ever since the night he had dinner with Lilly Cooper, he hadn't been able to get her off his mind. He was interested in her, and thought she might be interested in him too, although she gave no obvious signs of encouragement for anything else in the future. From what he observed, she seemed lonely, but not desperate. Maybe he was in the right place at the right time. He was curious and excited, wondering what Lilly was really like. She appeared reserved and polite. Was it just a thin veneer of aloofness or was she cold deep down, all the way to her heart?

Emboldened to impress her, throwing caution to the wind this time, he'd offered her his second-generation microchip—a new body and mind, a new chance in life. He made it clear she must be discreet and gave her his business card so she could call if she ever needed him.

He arranged for Gary, a cab driver that he often used, to

be on the lookout for her after that night at the restaurant. Gary watched Lilly and followed her for a couple of days to get an idea of her itinerary, routines, and travel patterns. Kite toyed with the idea of casually bumping into Lilly, but he didn't. He believed everything happened for a reason. And so he waited.

When she finally called, Kite told her he would send a taxi to pick her up and bring her to him. Rubbing the palms of his hands together in anticipation, he was overcome with excitement and joy. Fortunately, he had a new upgraded mind control microchip left from the last shipment on Monday for Lilly, the one with the purple label that reversed aging on a cellular level. He had already used the other two—injecting Gigi with the red-labeled microchip that cured her illness and Ellen with the blue-labeled one that controlled her weight. Today was Lilly's lucky day.

The taxi pulled up to the building. Gary glanced at the back seat, checking on his passenger. The doctor would be pleased. Gary knew how much he trusted him, and he was moving up the ranks fast. He put on his best smile and opened the car door for Lilly. She barely glanced at him, focusing her attention on the doctor instead.

Kite rushed to greet Lilly, taking her by the arm and nodding his thanks to Gary before escorting her inside his new office with its fresh white paint and hygienic, sterile-looking rooms. He opened this second location to garner new clients, the paying kind. The sordid warehouse had served its purpose. It would be closing soon with the impending success of the second- generation microchip.

As Lilly lay on the table, the doctor took his time, pulling over his tray and explaining the procedure. The injection pen had been loaded up with the upgraded mind control chip Lilly demanded once he explained it could give her body the youth she'd lost and drive out the bitterness that lingered after the divorce, freeing her from the past and releasing her to start a new life. The timing was perfect. In his eagerness to give her what she needed, what she insisted on getting now, he also skipped the trial period with an end date like the one he'd programmed into Ellen's chip.

Chapter 14

ELLEN

Ellen pranced around, reluctant to take off her new dress. The longer she wore it, the happier she felt. She bent to touch her toes. No problem. She hadn't been able to do that for ages. She couldn't wait to buy new clothes—nothing in her closet fit now. She called her mom, managing a quick winded, "Hi, Mom."

"Hey Elly, I'm so glad you called."

"Yeah, Mom." At first, her Mom was the only one who called her Elly and got away with it. When the kids found out, they teased her mercilessly at school. "Elly the hilly… has a big belly." The taunts were hurtful and she never forgot them. She begged her Mom to stop calling her Elly. *Please mom, please stop!* But she never did. She was stuck on calling her Elly and never changed it. "Hey, you've got my room ready for next week? You know I'm coming home for the wedding."

"Oh hon, we thought you'd be coming. But your cousin said she mailed you the wedding invitation three weeks ago."

She paused. "Have you sent back your RSVP?"

"Sorry, Mom, I forgot. I'll send it tomorrow."

"I told her you were busy and to please save you a place in case you forgot to mail it." She sighed, irritated at her flighty daughter. "You know, if it wasn't for your cousin, you wouldn't be getting a seat at the reception dinner."

"Err, well… thanks, Mom."

"Be sure to get a nice—I mean, a *very* nice gift for your cousin."

"Okay, I will. See you next weekend."

Ending the call, Ellen picked up her slim new pink pen and added *get a very nice gift* to her to-do list before the wedding. She didn't want to tell her Mom yet about her new look. The thought of surprising her in person was worth the wait.

Chapter 15
GIGI

Something was bugging Steve after the call with Rex. He was old enough to be his father, but they were good friends. Steve had envied Rex the first time he met Gigi. She was in her early twenties, and he couldn't believe how gorgeous and nice she was. Surely they were dating? But Rex assured him they were only roommates and were seeing other people.

Steve could tell something was worrying Rex the moment he spoke. The thing that happened to Gigi was weird, out of the blue and so out of character.

After Rex told him where Gigi was found, he had gone to the hotel and talked the staff into letting him see the security camera tapes. Sure enough, she appeared on them. He had rewound it back to the time shortly before she called Rex. The tapes showed her in the hotel lobby at that time. It was just as Rex said, even the details. What puzzled him was the camera footage before she got there. It was angled, not facing the elevator, so there wasn't a good shot of the doors opening when Gigi came into the lobby. He caught a blur of three people walking across the room, two men with Gigi in the middle. He would have to figure out some other way to find out who brought her in the hotel.

52

Chapter 16
DR. KITE

KITE MADE A FEW NOTES. Right now things were going well. The hiccup had been Gigi. He toyed over the possibilities. Sometimes the modern microchips malfunctioned, but that was so rare, and it hadn't been a problem yet. Or the person may have reacted to it for some other reason. He had gotten a new batch of upgraded microchips a few days ago, the ones with the mind control, and they came in three tubes that were color labeled—red, blue, and purple. For Gigi, he'd picked red, the same color as the original microchip that cured her tinnitus.

Since the early days, Kite used loners or vagrants who wouldn't be easily traced or missed by family as test subjects. In his desperation to succeed, he experimented on involuntary human subjects, violating the ethics of human experimentation.

Obsessed, he had devoured every piece of scientific literature, taking special interest in another company that showed early promise in the research of implantable microchips. But after unacceptable risks and side effects came to light, that company abandoned its research. Kite persisted, his curiosity and intellect challenged. Years of meticulous experiments bore no fruit until, one day, pure luck brought a chance discovery. He made arrangements with an offshore laboratory to make the chips. This led to the first generation of implantable microchips that altered physical aspects.

He had developed three prototypes distinguished by red, blue, and purple labels—one to cure illnesses and heal injuries, one to re-sculpture and lose fat, and one to rejuvenate and reverse the aging process. The second-generation of microchips took it a step further, incorporating advanced technology to alter the mind. This phase of the project was the most challenging. He was at the point of giving up when he came across the renegade microchip. Instead of tossing it, he studied it to figure out how the renegade took over the person's mind.

This upgraded chip was to be an improvement over the first, by adding mind control in sync with the body's changes to fortify the mind-body connection. If this worked, his next improved model would be a nanochip, incredibly tiny yet powerful, and specifically programmed to target cells with unparalleled speed and precision. He savored the thought of releasing an army of nanobots, not only to seek and kill cells, but also to replace and replicate—even itself.

Chapter 17

LILLY

THE DIVORCE LEFT ITS MARK on Lilly, turning her into a bitter and angry woman. She had devoted her whole life to Frank, helping him build his business. She didn't have any kids—Frank was absolutely firm that he didn't want any. Every time she thought of Frank, her fingers inevitably flexed into a claw-like grasp. She would have dug out Frank's eyes if she could. How dare he take the best years of her life and all she offered, then get rid of her after she helped him achieve his goals? He couldn't have done any of it without her.

The night she was at the restaurant, Lilly was contemplating her fate. She wanted revenge. Frank was stingy with her in the divorce, and she had to fight for every penny. Frank wasn't going to give it to her otherwise. She clung to the bitterness, fueling her regret at the years wasted on that man.

Now that she was divorced, even her freedom failed to provide solace. No longer would she have to spend hours worrying about Frank's business. Funny, that should have been a clue… it was always *Frank's*, never Frank *and* Lilly's. He never referred to it that way when he talked, and her name wasn't on the website, the business card, or anywhere else. Now she understood why he acted that way—he wanted to keep it all to himself. That should have been a warning sign. She had asked him often, but he so effortlessly brushed away her requests with a noncommittal remark.

If only she hadn't been so trusting, if she hadn't been so focused on the business, she might have noticed that he was dallying with that fool girl, his office assistant. He was still cautious before the divorce—Lilly guessed he didn't want to lose it all to her. Afterward, she heard he married that girl and they had a baby. Imagine that, Frank who *never* wanted kids. Instead, she was bringing him another mouth to feed. Lilly shook her head.

At the restaurant, Lilly had been in a foul mood before Kite arrived. She stewed as she settled in and ordered dinner. But as she sipped the wine and tasted the fine food, her frosty exterior gradually warmed as the craving and emptiness in her stomach eased. She started to feel better.

Lilly had just ordered coffee and dessert when the hostess, Sally, arrived at her table with Kite in tow. Sally's usual upbeat manner turned flustered when she saw Lilly.

"Sally, it's okay," said Lilly softly, so only Sally could hear. "It's not a big deal. There's room for two at this table. I don't bite."

Truth be told, Kite wasn't bad company. The man liked to talk, and she let him. Oh, how he went on and on. But it was pleasant. She made a slight effort to engage in small talk.

But she didn't expect too much. After all, they were just sharing a table. If things had turned sour, she was prepared to make an excuse and dash out, taking the dessert to go.

Luckily that didn't happen. She let Kite babble on and on. He apparently thought she was enjoying the conversation.

But she was tuning him out a little at a time. One had to be careful with this charade. You could nod every once in a while to give the impression that you've heard and understand what your table companion was saying. But if you nodded at an inappropriate time, or affirmed something that was said but you had no clue to what it was, you could get into trouble. And then, there's the yawn. That had worked too. She could throw her head back, for effect, and give a long slow yawn, also for effect. Add a few shoulder shrugs and then gestures to gather her things to go while stifling another yawn, then muttering, "I really must go. It's past my bedtime." This trick usually generated jokes from the unsuspecting other party about bedtime for a full-grown woman. Nothing like leaving the other party laughing.

Chapter 18
GIGI

The worst thing was the waiting.

Gigi was thankful to have Rex by her side. It made the whole ordeal bearable. If he hadn't made that call to Steve, they wouldn't have found her car before it was towed away. She knew how lucky she was to have survived—with not even a scrape or broken bone in her body. She felt like the luckiest girl alive, grateful to God she hadn't been seriously injured, paralyzed, or worse. Had she driven on the road and swerved toward the wall because of a deer or a squirrel, or something else? Had she fallen asleep and woken up at the last minute in time to avert a head-on crash? Or—the unthinkable—had she *wanted* to run straight into the wall? She might never know if she couldn't remember the accident, but she did realize she had a second chance in life.

The night before the accident, in her dreams, she had almost crossed over to the other side and was hanging by a rope over the precipice. Then she heard someone calling her, "Gigi, wake up!" She must have cried out in her sleep in her fear of falling over the edge.

When she opened her eyes, Rex was leaning over her bed, the loose tendrils of his shoulder-length hair tickling her face as he shook her.

"You're having some badass nightmare." His face had looked funny, scrunched with concern and fear.

"Yeah."

"Those nightmares. Are they new?"

"Yes, they started recently," said Gigi, and she went on to describe the terrifying new dreams that started a few nights ago at the time the new mind control chip was implanted. Her explanation stopped here—she never told Rex about her treatment by Kite and the chip. He didn't know.

"No wonder you screamed."

"I was scared shitless, it seemed so real." Gigi laughed nervously. "I could see it, my breath frosting in the cold. I could feel it, the wind blowing, swaying me as I held on to the rope over the precipice… the dark void below." She gulped. "It felt so real—so frightening. I thought I'd die right then and there."

Rex had comforted her that night in the best way he could. Keeping his voice low, soothing, and calming, he held her in his arms as he felt her muscles gradually relax, letting go of the tension. She had experienced extreme fear, so real and inescapable. Her body had been in a fight-or-flight mode and frozen. If it had gotten any worse, he worried that she'd have a heart attack. They say you can die of fright, and he believed there was truth to that.

"There, there," said Rex. "Shh… shh." He gently rocked her back and forth. Her fearful state reminded him of a frightened rabbit with its eyes fixated in terror, held in the headlights of an oncoming car. Frozen in mid-stride, unable to move, unable to save itself from the crushing weight of the car as it rushed closer, bringing death.

Chapter 19

ELLEN

THE PLANE TAXIED DOWN TO the end of the runway, next in line to go. The flaps on the wings made a whirring sound as they opened. Ellen re-checked her seat belt. She chewed her gum furiously, sitting back in her seat with her eyes closed, bracing as the engine revved and the plane prepared to take off.

Airborne, she heard the mechanical sounds of the wheels retracting and the wing flaps closing back up as the plane gained attitude, finally reaching cruising speed. In a few hours, she would be back at the family home and in her old bedroom. She focused on that. She took a deep breath, keeping her eyes shut, and settled in for the trip.

"What would you like to drink, sir?" asked the flight attendant, speaking to the guy in the aisle seat. Ellen was barely awake when she heard this. She briefly considered forgoing the drink and pretzels to keep on dozing. She had a few seconds to decide before the man next to her would be served and the cart would start moving down the aisle. If she kept her eyes closed, they wouldn't disturb her.

Hearing the drop of ice cubes in the cup, the fizz of the can opening, and the rattling of cubes as the guy drank, Ellen sat up. The stewardess smiled and asked the same question. "What would you like to drink?"

"I'll have tonic water, please," said Ellen as she pulled the tray table down.

"Pretzel?"

"Yes, please."

The stewardess handed her a pack before pushing the cart along.

Ellen looked over the pretzel package, but couldn't find the little tear mark. "Cheap shit," she muttered under her breath. "Cheap fucking shit."

"May I give you a hand?" said the guy sitting next to her, who had been watching all this with a bemused look.

Oh God no, he's heard me cursing. Slipping an embarrassed glance at the smartly dressed man, Ellen couldn't help blushing and thinking, *What a cute guy.* "Sure, give it a try if you like," said Ellen as she handed it to him with a coy smile. No harm in trying to repair the damage.

He didn't bother looking for the notches, just gripped the packet with both hands and tore it open with a practiced smooth motion. "Here," he said with a grin. "Enjoy your pretzels."

"I sure lucked out sitting next to Mr. Superman," said Ellen. Remembering her manners, she said, "Okay, let's start over. Hi, I'm Ellen."

"I'm Brad," he said. "Nice to meet you."

"You have a way with pretzels, you know."

"And you have a way with men."

"Are you hitting on me?"

"Only if you say so."

She laughed. "Okay, let's start over *again*. I'm Ellen, and I am traveling to Woodville to attend my cousin's wedding."

"Hi, I'm Brad, and I have a stopover at Woodville before catching a plane to Denver for a business meeting."

"What line of work are you in?"

"Investment, real estate, and a bit of import-export."

"Business good these days?"

"Yes, right now real estate markets are flooded with foreign investors coming here to buy property. Real estate is a safer bet."

"You travel a lot?"

"A little too much sometimes. My home is here. I've got a place on the north side."

"I live here too. I have an apartment in the city. Close to everything."

"You like what you do?"

"Most days. You know it's crazy sometimes. I'm good at what I do. I'm an administrative assistant."

"We all have to make a living somehow," said Brad. "Unless you're independently wealthy or you win the lottery."

Ellen laughed. Sweet dreams. At first look, Brad seemed really young, but she guessed he was a little bit older, maybe in his early thirties. Very well-groomed, clean-shaven, a nice crew cut, and an aftershave with a subtle scent of virile masculinity.

She wanted to ask Brad outright what he used as aftershave, but decided she'd steer the conversation elsewhere first. "You know, my dad was an aftershave guy, and he used the same brand for over thirty years."

Brad lifted an eyebrow, brown eyes curious.

"He refused to try a different brand, even when we bought him other ones for his birthday presents," said Ellen. "Do you think men are more loyal or less adventurous?"

"You're asking about aftershave or men in general?"

"Hmm… aftershave, but yeah."

"I personally think men are mostly creatures of habit. My dad was the same way, he used the same aftershave for years too," said Brad with a twinkle in his eyes. "I used to try his when I was a kid. I'd climb up on the bathroom counter top to reach the cabinet door to get it. He always kept it in the same place too." He paused, shaking his head, then continued. "Once when I grabbed that blue bottle, it slipped out of my tiny hands, smashing on the floor. I was mortified. My mind whipped through all kinds of scenarios of what my dad would do to punish me."

"Uh oh, then what happened? Did he beat you?"

Reflecting for a moment, Brad said, "As luck would have it, my mom was in the bedroom when it happened. She heard the bottle shatter, and me bawling my eyes out. She rushed over and held me until my crying stopped, then helped clean it up. We headed over to the nearest store and got another one. My dad never found out about it."

"Your mom spared you from his punishment."

"Yup, and I learned my lesson," said Brad, a bit of pride

sneaking into his voice. "And I paid my mom back out of my paper boy earnings."

"I like your mom," said Ellen with a nod.

The rest of the flight went too quickly, as they chatted and laughed the rest of the way. After the plane landed, they parted ways, but not before they had exchanged phone numbers and made plans for dinner in a week, when they were both back home.

Chapter 20
LILLY

"Watch your step, ma'am," said Gary, holding the umbrella over Lilly's head as she stepped out of the cab. Overhead, the raindrops spattered big clumpy drops and the thunder roared. Gary had parked the taxi close to the sidewalk in front of her home so he could walk her up the steps to the front door of her brick townhouse. She told him she hated days like this and didn't have an umbrella.

Gary loved the rain, whether watching from inside the house or being outside in it. He didn't mind getting wet at all. As a child, he used to play a game, counting the seconds between the lightning flash and thunder clap, and making a big dip of his hands, like a conductor with his baton, when he timed the clap of thunder just right. He played it so many times it became his favorite pastime when it rained.

Today the gods were angry and wouldn't let up. When the clouds grew dark and pulled the curtain over the sky, he knew it'd be a fierce storm, like the weatherman predicted. Not a quick summer storm that blew over almost as soon as it started. This one was loud, angry, demanding, and full of raging sparks and forceful energy. The rain pelted mercilessly, not slowing down. The wind added its chorus to the thunder and blew gusts that toppled signs, downed trees, and lifted anything it could move or carry in its path.

Gary guided Lilly across the pavement and up the steps of her townhouse, shielding her with his body and deflecting the rain with the umbrella. When the lightning flashed, Gary was so intent on counting the seconds until the thunder that he took his eyes off Lilly for a moment. As the gods would have it, it was perfectly timed so that a mighty gust of wind inverted the umbrella and almost sent it flying out of his grip. Instantly, a torrent of rain came down hard on Lilly's head, catching her by surprise as it pelted water on her face and shoulders. The metal ribs of the umbrella flapped helplessly, slapping more water on her.

In a flash, she turned around to face Gary, her features contorted, ugly and demonic. Growling, Lilly uttered a deep, guttural sound—chilling and feral.

Before Gary could react, Lilly savagely pushed him. He teetered on the edge of the step, trying to catch his balance, desperately gripping the umbrella and impervious to the rain that soaked his clothes. At that moment in time, in an instant that seemed like an eternity, he looked desperately into Lilly's eyes—then he toppled, falling backwards, slipping down the concrete steps until his head hit the pavement. Gary lay crumpled on the sidewalk, his leg bent at an awkward angle, blood pouring out of his head like red juice seeping from a cracked melon.

Lilly looked down from the top of the steps, her eyes triumphant. The implanted chip had fixed her moods, calmed her anger and bitterness after the divorce. But in the instant that Gary failed to shelter her from the rain, all her pent-up rage at men momentarily returned, resulting in her pushing him viciously away—exacting her ultimate revenge, killing him. It was an extreme reaction—a moment of deep, uncontrollable anger. She wondered, *was it a display of her chip gone bad or did it become an instrument to release her deepest desire, her dark evil within?*

The cab door was still open, the engine running, and the wipers going, not missing a beat. Lilly turned around, unlocked her front door, and walked inside, never looking back.

Chapter 21
DR. KITE

ON THE OTHER SIDE OF town, Kite stood by his office window, watching the rain and the powerful storm raging outside. He preferred to be dry and inside on a day like this. No need to go out unless it was an emergency. From the comfort of his office, he watched the raindrops hitting the window and rolling down in steady streams. As a new drop flowed, it added to the stream, sometimes changing the course of it. He was so absorbed that he didn't hear the knock on the door. When the knock came again, this time louder and more insistent, he reluctantly turned around. "Come in."

Daman opened the door. He held a package in his hands. "New delivery, boss. This just came."

Kite could see it was stamped with the word *Urgent* in red letters. This was unusual. The delivery already came last Monday, and he wasn't expecting another one. He took the package quickly and ripped it open. He nodded dismissively to the kid, at the same time thanking him.

Inside the well-padded package was the usual black box. However, this time a neatly typed note was attached to the outside of the box. It simply said, "Problem on Monday's package. Two out of three mind control chips defective."

Kite slowly closed the container. He stared at it, eyes wide open, as the horror started to sink in.

Oh, God no. What have I done?

Chapter 22

GIGI

STEVE CAUGHT SIGHT OF THE clock, irritably thinking, *Damn, it's getting late.* He had been so wrapped up in his work that time slipped by. All afternoon he had been watching the videotapes of the hotel parking garage. He poured over each one, checking the arrivals and departures of the vehicles to and from the parking deck, zooming in to see the drivers' and passengers' faces. It was a painstaking, slow process. He sat in his chair, frustrated and annoyed. By process of elimination, Steve ruled out the ones that didn't coincide with Gigi's arrival and cross-checked the rest against the roster of hotel guest's vehicles until he narrowed it down to a few. He wasn't able to see Gigi in any of the close-up frames of the inside of the vehicles. That didn't surprise him.

Rex had left Steve a voice mail to tell him they saw Gigi's car at the highway underpass before it was towed away, thanking him profusely. Steve felt a twinge of guilt that he hadn't had a chance to call him back. Perhaps it was better to wait until tomorrow. He may have more news then.

Steve stood up, holding the cup of cold, stale coffee in his hands. It was bad coffee to begin with. He had to be really desperate to drink that all afternoon. As a matter of fact, he didn't even have lunch. He made it through the day on coffee, candy, and junk food. A nice, hot home-cooked meal sounded very enticing now. But wait—he didn't have anyone at home waiting for him with a hot meal. He crushed the paper coffee cup and tossed it into the trash can along with the wrappers of his junk food. Tonight he would stop by the diner and treat himself to a nice meal.

Tomorrow would be another day.

Chapter 23

ELLEN

"I NOW PRONOUNCE YOU HUSBAND and wife. You may kiss the bride," said the pastor. The organ music filled the church as the exuberant couple dashed outside, the guests tossing pink flower petals for a sweet send-off.

Ellen wiped away a few happy tears. She wished with all her heart that one day she would find happiness like this to last a lifetime. And kids, well she loved kids, and wanted to start her own family soon.

She had buried this ache deep down inside her somewhere. She took solace with each bite, snuffing her dreams as the pounds and the inches crept up with each year that rolled by. She nursed every hurt and every pain with more food.

Food became the answer to everything. It was the healer, better than medicine. It was there at every occasion, every celebration. It was everywhere. Food became her interest, her necessity, and her obsession.

When she had an opportunity to choose, she chose food.

As she looked back on happy occasions when her friends and relatives celebrated weddings and births, every regret became replaced by food. Ellen didn't choose good food or bad food—it didn't matter. Food was what she could stuff in her mouth. It was sweet, it was spicy, it was salty, it was zesty. It was soft, it was crunchy, it was hard, it was solid, it was juicy.

It didn't matter.

She managed to lose some weight. She went on diets and worked so hard. Then she celebrated her success with food and gained back every pound that she'd lost. She did this again and again. And she noticed the older she got, the more easily she put on weight and the harder it was to lose it.

One day at work, she overheard some people making jokes about a fat woman when she stepped in the break room to microwave her lunch. Then she realized later they were talking about her. She was mortified. It was all she could do to make it through the day with her head held high. When she got home, she cried.

From that day forward, she watched every bite, counted calories, and managed to lose thirty-five pounds. She was determined to get her body back, and in the process, get her life back. She knew there had to be more to life than this— toiling away at the office, eating when she was upset, eating to take away the hurt. But the last thirty pounds were the hardest, and she couldn't get rid of them herself.

Kite had provided a lifeline. She took this new chance in life and grabbed it. Her time had come, and she was ready. This trip to her cousin's wedding was just the start. Grunting with satisfaction, Ellen replayed the clips in her mind—her

Mom left speechless (for once), her family and her cousin's family's stunned looks, and her friends' compliments at the wedding.

Ellen's thoughts turned to Brad on the plane. She really enjoyed herself, and the flirting came naturally. Men had always found her face attractive, and she retained her beauty and youthful appearance. But it had been a very long time since someone paid her much attention. When she saw him again, she would make up for lost time. She still had hopes that her life could be more than what it was today, the hope of love. No promises, no expectations, just taking life one day at a time. Who knows what could happen? Life is what it is.

A spark flew—that was for sure. And it wasn't just her. Ellen saw it in Brad's warm brown eyes, sensed he was just as interested in her as she was in him.

Chapter 24

GIGI

REX NOTICED THAT GIGI WAS still a bit off. He had chalked it up to the trauma of the accident and her stress over it. He was worried about her and wanted to be sure that she wasn't going to go off the deep end or do something crazy. He checked in on her often while she was sleeping. Gigi had refused all medical treatments and insisted that she was all right. Rex didn't want to force her. If all she needed was time, time was what he would give her. Rex was a patient man. As he sat down with a cup of morning coffee, his cell phone rang.

"Hey Rex, got your message. How are you doing?"

"Oh, hey Steve. Man, I slept like a rock."

"And Gigi?"

"Slept through the night. I put a baby monitor in Gigi's room in case she woke up with another nightmare."

"So she's getting better?"

"Well, physically she is." He took a sip of his coffee. "I just hope her nightmares don't come back."

"Maybe it's time to take her to the doctor."

"She doesn't want to go yet. Hey, did you find out anything from the hotel parking cameras?"

"I was just about to update you on that," said Steve after a brief pause. "I've been able to narrow it down, and I'm checking the registrations now. My guess is one of these may lead to something. You're sure Gigi doesn't remember how she got to the hotel?"

"Not really. The only thing she said was she thought it was dark and she may have been lying down. She heard faint voices, but nothing that she could identify. And no details on the vehicles or anything else."

"Maybe she was blindfolded in the back, or in a van? If you find out anything else let me know."

"Yup, talk to you later."

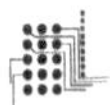

Steve got back to his computer. There were two vehicles that he had questions about. The car tags on the camera didn't match the information in the system. The first vehicle was a black SUV. The owner's name and the registration showed a male and female with different last names.

He placed a call to the first person listed. "Hello, my name is Steve Cosine, and I'm a consultant looking into this. Your SUV popped up with a different name on the owner and the registration. Are you the owner?"

"What's this about? Am—am I in some kinda trouble?" said the guy who answered the phone.

"I'm trying to track down a vehicle that may have been involved in an accident. Is this your car?"

"We haven't gotten around to changing the information."

"So you are the owner?"

"*Was*—I got divorced and the wife, the ex-wife, well, she got the car."

"So you don't have the keys either?"

"I gave her the car when the divorce became final a few days ago, and that's when I gave her my keys. She was going to get the title changed to her name first."

"Were you driving the vehicle at the Hotel Seven or was it your ex-wife?"

"I didn't go there."

"Any reason for your ex-wife to be there?"

"Yeah, I think so. She's an event coordinator—books rooms, handles food, drinks, and all those details. You could easily confirm that with the hotel."

Satisfied, Steve concluded by saying, "This will do for now. Thanks for your cooperation."

Steve spoke with his contact at the hotel, and it all checked out.

Now, he skipped to the last name he had circled and put a question mark next to it. The vehicle was a white van registered in a man's name. He made a note of the address and decided to go in person to check it out. The location was in a dilapidated part of town, run-down and a little seedy. Steve knocked on the door. Hearing no sound, he pounded, this time much louder. He definitely heard something—voices, and the sound of chairs being pushed.

Finally, he heard a female voice and the door opened. "Hello," she said cautiously.

"I'm looking for Raul. Is he here?"

She looked over her shoulder and shouted, "Raul?"

An old man limped from the back room.

Steve held up a photo of the white van. "Is this your van?"

Raul's eyes lit up. "You found it?"

"Is this your van? Where is it?"

"I don't know. It looks like my white van, but it was stolen," stuttered Raul.

"Did you report it?"

Raul hesitated.

Maybe there was some reason he was holding back. Steve softened his voice. "Look, I'm not here to get you in trouble with the authorities. I just want to know about your vehicle. It may have been involved in an accident."

Raul relaxed and shook his head. But he insisted, "I don't know."

It was clear he didn't know who stole his vehicle, and he was too afraid to report it once it was stolen. Track this vehicle down and likely Steve would find the abductors.

Chapter 25
ELLEN

ELLEN COULD HARDLY WAIT FOR the plane to land. She was so looking forward to coming home, and the thought of seeing Brad again made her feel like a giddy girl with a high school crush. An image of Brad popped up—a tall, handsome dude with a perfectly toned body and muscles that other men envied. Well, it took a *bit* of imagination seeing how Ellen had only seen him with his shirt on. Brad had texted her after the wedding, and they firmed up their plans to get together tonight for dinner. He was such a gentleman, insisting on picking her up. For a moment she wished he'd bring her a corsage and take her to the prom. She, Ellen, on Brad's arm. All eyes on them.

Ellen checked the clock on the dashboard while she was driving home from work. She had two and a half hours to get home, take a shower, and get ready. He said he'd be picking her up at 6:00 p.m. She had gotten off work a little early to avoid the rush-hour traffic, which was particularly bad on a Friday. She was able to whiz home in no time at all. After a quick shower, she put on a little red dress that she had picked up on the trip in anticipation of the date. It was tight-fitting and flattered her shape in all the right places. She was pleased.

Ellen heard the knock on the door. Brad was right on time. She took one last look at herself in the mirror, admiring the way her backside looked, before going to open the door.

"Well, *hello* Ellen." Brad gave a long whistle when he saw her.

Blushing, she gave him a quick welcoming hug. "Brad."

Brad held her for a second longer before releasing her.

"So, where're we going?" Ellen said.

"It's a surprise," he said with a laugh.

"I'm assuming you've got as much good taste in food as women?" she teased.

"I'll let you be the judge of that."

Ellen laughed heartily as they walked to his car, at ease with the banter.

The new seafood restaurant was the rave of town, and she had actually read the reviews. It was stunning, decorated in various tones of blue, all artfully done to give the impression that you were in an ocean—in the deep blue sea. At any moment, you almost expected to meet a mermaid or a school of fish. Stepping into the restaurant was like entering another world ruled by Neptune.

The food was delicious, skillfully prepared with the freshest of seafood. For starters, Ellen had the strawberry spinach salad with crumbled seaweed chips. Brad had the chilled shrimp cocktail with red chili cocktail sauce. For the entrée, hers was the restaurant's signature raw oysters with Russian caviar, his was the seared sea scallops with ginger lime sauce.

They took their time with the meal, stretching out the delightful evening. Ellen enjoyed every bit of it. After making their way through salad, appetizer, and the entrée, there was no room for dessert, so they ordered coffee and talked.

On the way back, as Brad drove, Ellen lay in the seat and almost purred. Brad turned to look at her. "That good, huh?"

"You weren't kidding about that place."

He grinned sheepishly. "And who said I have great taste?"

She pushed his arm playfully. "Take me home."

"At your service," he said with a salute.

They joked and teased all the way to her apartment.

Brad parked, got out, and went around to open her door for her.

Ellen thought, *every bit a gentleman.* "Would you like some dessert now?"

"If you're making good coffee…"

"Nothing but the best in this house," said Ellen as she turned the key. Brad was right behind her—his hand brushing against her arm when he reached out to hold the door open. She quivered at his touch, so light and electrifying.

As soon as they got inside, she slammed the door shut and kicked off her shoes. Brad moved closer and she stepped forward, her chin up, her lips parting slightly, her eyes beckoning as he searched for her response. Cupping her face in his hands, his lips brushed hers gently. She responded with a greater sense of urgency. They kissed passionately, lips locking. When they broke for air, he whispered hoarsely in her ear, "Are you my dessert?"

Laughing between kisses, she pushed him down the hallway to her bedroom, shedding her clothing along the way. They flopped on the bed, Brad on top. Ellen felt athletic, lithe, and free as she moved, swayed, and curved around Brad. His body matched hers, in movement and in playfulness. Ellen hooked her leg around Brad for leverage and flipped over easily. She became the lead, directing and guiding. They did a quick dance, passionate and playful.

As Ellen nuzzled his ear and tickled the hairs on his chest, moving down to between his legs and the really long curly hairs there, Brad groaned, his body announcing he was ready for another dance.

They started slowly this time, gently touching, exploring each other's body to find all the right steps and movements. He easily clasped his hands around her slim waist and lifted her up before positioning her on top. Soon they were both almost out of breath, reaching that final exquisite crescendo. At that moment, Ellen caught a glimpse of the time on her digital clock—8:30. Ellen was still on top, and Brad had his eyes closed—but in that instant, her body changed.

Brad clasped his hands around Ellen's waist again, but instead of a smooth, slim waist, his fingers grasped flesh—rolls of flesh like dough that he could dig his fingers into.

His mind refused to comprehend what his hands were telling him. As his part shriveled and his head started to clear, Brad kept his eyes closed as he moved his hands slowly up and down her back. He stopped, freezing at her butt. He slowly flattened his palms, expanding his fingers as wide as they could go, first to one side, then the other, measuring the span of her butt in disbelief.

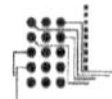

Ellen was in pure ecstasy when they reached the crescendo together. She almost lost her mind. But in that same instant, as her whole body quaked in tandem with Brad's—it changed. With a sickening feeling, she felt her body expand and become heavy. Heavy like she gained back the thirty pounds she had lost and more.

Chapter 26

GIGI

WHEN SHE FINALLY REMEMBERED, GIGI knew why she'd rather be dead. It became all too clear to her. The events of the past few days were no longer a void.

Gigi had a condition, tinnitus, a ringing and sometimes a buzzing sound in her ears. At first, she tried to ignore it as the noise came and went intermittently, albeit occasionally at the most inconvenient or embarrassing circumstances.

She tried to live with it, managing it as it appeared, hiding it from people. Gradually, the sounds became louder, more persistent, and present for longer periods of time. Day and night, the noise in her head affected her waking and sleeping hours, keeping her up most of the night.

Tortured by her condition, Gigi sought out doctors, but they could never find the cause. She tried their treatments. Some temporarily masked the symptoms or provided limited relief, but none could cure this condition. She couldn't get the noise out of her head, and feared she would go crazy living with this.

Frantic, out of options, and desperate, she heard through the grapevine about a doctor who was whispered to be quite unconventional and secretive. She arranged for a visit through contacts and was picked up by Kite's cab driver at a predestined location. Then she was blindfolded and taken to see Kite, where he swore her to secrecy before implanting the first-generation microchip. It was her last-ditch effort after everything she tried had failed. She was determined not to give up.

She went back to see Kite last Monday after he received the new shipment, and he replaced her original microchip with an upgraded one. That was in the morning. Her terrifying nightmares started that night, then the car accident a few days later.

Gigi had blocked out the trauma of the accident. She dreaded reliving it, not wanting to face the truth. The new nightmares had been real. They were as much a part of her life as anything. She couldn't even begin to describe the terror and the depth of pull she felt. Every waking hour she dreaded the nights. She tried to fight it as hard as she could, thinking, *I could beat it.* But as time went on, the nightmares and the pull to the other side became stronger and stronger, until it reached a crescendo—as her car hurled toward the concrete wall.

In the last few months, it became clear to her how much Rex meant to her. He was her comforter, protector, best friend, the person she'd call if she had one last call to make. Rex stuck with her, helping her to cope and deal with her illness. Her whole life changed with the tinnitus, but having him there made all the difference.

Seeing his actions throughout this ordeal and realizing the very essence of his soul stirred something deep inside her—at the instant when it mattered, as she confronted the fragility of life and released the courage that was within her.

His love gave her the strength to live, and she fought to survive. But now she wanted more, and with the tinnitus and nightmares gone, she was ready. She needed to tell Rex, and he needed to hear the truth now. She picked up her pen.

*My dear Rex—I **never** gave up. What I can tell you is how it felt, like a switch had been turned and my time was up. My body went through the motions and I couldn't stop it. It was as if I was on autopilot. The near-crash was no accident. I was headed toward the wall, a certain death.*

I can't explain why it didn't happen except to say that at the last moment a part of me wouldn't surrender to it and, with every bit of fierce strength that I had left, I somehow wrenched the wheel, changing the path. A few days before, the new nightmares came with an intensity and depth that was more frightening than any I've ever experienced. I didn't want to fall down the precipice to the darkness below. I tried so hard to fight it. You were by my side. But each day, the pull became stronger and stronger, bringing me closer to the wall, right up to the accident.

I've got a second chance to live now. Perhaps one day we'll be lovers. I'd like that.
Gigi

Chapter 27

DR. KITE

KITE LOOKED UP AS THE light blinked during the storm. He sighed, rubbing his eyes. The defect in two of the three chips was a cruel twist. He didn't know for sure who had received those. He shook his head. Wearily, he entered a comment in the system for each of the three names—Gigi, Ellen, Lilly: INAPPROPRIATE SUBJECT FOR IMPLANTS. REMOVE DEFECTIVE UPGRADE CHIP.

He had replaced Gigi's chip already. Reaching for his cell phone, it rang before he could make a call to arrange the other removals.

"Hello?"

"Warehouse burning…" said the other man on the line.

"*What?* Say that again!"

"Burned… struck by lightning."

"No, oh no!" said Kite repeatedly as he listened to catch every word uttered by the frantic, blubbering man on the other end.

"Called 911?"

"Yeah, line was flooded."

"Did you try calling the fire department?"

"Couldn't get through in time, fire trucks out…"

"In the storm?"

"Got here too late…"

Kite tapped his cell phone abruptly, ending the call in mid-sentence. All of his work, destroyed. He gripped the phone, wanting to throw it, to smash it into smithereens.

Chapter 28
LILLY

THE STORM THAT TOOK THE city wreaked havoc and left devastation in its path. The governor had declared a state of emergency. Sirens could be heard wailing most of the day. The exhausted fire and police were stretched thin. Volunteers helped in the rescue. In the hours that transpired, the death of Gary was counted as another casualty of the storm. Lilly was questioned and released. There were no witnesses.

Epilogue

A YEAR LATER

Chapter 29
ELLEN

KNOCK, KNOCK.

"Mom, thanks for coming over tonight," said Ellen, opening her door.

Brushing a kiss on Ellen's cheek as she walked in, her mom was carrying a large green tote. "I picked up some groceries on the way."

"I couldn't have done it alone without your help these last three months."

"That's why your dad and I moved down here, Elly."

"Yeah, and I am so glad you did—*Grandma*."

Walking to the nursery, Grandma pulled out the newest toy she had brought, a soft puffamuffin penguin. Chuckling to the baby in the crib, she reached in with a practiced hand. "Now let me hold my little Angie."

"Mom," said Ellen as she leaned over to tuck in a corner of the blanket, making sure Angie was snuggly wrapped. "I'm so happy now… so thoroughly in love with my baby."

"She's so beautiful."

"Angie's the best thing that's ever happened to me, and I have Brad to thank for it."

"I thought… isn't Brad's out of the picture? You're a single mom now."

"Yes, but if it wasn't for him I wouldn't have Angie."

"Well, you sure know how to pick them. She's got his genes and good looks too."

"I did something else right this time," said Ellen as she smoothed her hands down her size eight slacks. After she got over the shock that followed the last scene with Brad, when her weight instantly jumped back up and then she found out she was pregnant, Ellen channeled all her determination into transforming her body, not just for herself but also for the new life she was carrying. She started small, cutting out bread, sugary snacks, and sodas. She ate healthy meals but smaller portions. She cut out meats and fried foods. She ate folate-rich foods. She walked a lot and did prenatal workouts. She changed her attitude. There was no going back once she started, fueled with new life and her energy.

"Are those new pants?"

"Yeah, Mom. I'm down another size and have kept my weight off since I had Angie. I did it this time, my way."

"I'm so proud of you—Ellen!"

"You just keep calling me Ellen. I hate it when you call me Elly."

"I'm sorry…"

"Forget the past. Elly is gone."

"I've never seen you happier."

"I know, Mom, *I know.*"

Chapter 30

LILLY

*K*NOCK, *KNOCK.*

Lilly was in the kitchen making a pot of fresh coffee when she heard the knock. She glanced up at the clock. It was 10:00 a.m., and she wasn't expecting anyone. *Who could it be?* With a sigh of irritation, she snatched a towel and quickly wiped her hands dry.

"Be just a minute," she yelled.

Opening the door, she found a stranger standing on her doorstep. It was a man dressed in a frumpy shirt with a slightly crooked tie.

"Excuse me," the man said, as he straightened his tie with one hand. "Are you Mrs. Cooper?"

She gave him her cool look, accompanied with a cooler and somewhat imperious tone as she demanded, "And who is asking?"

He cleared his throat. "Ma'am, I'm Steve Cosine. I'm a consultant on an insurance investigation."

"You must have the wrong house," she said, ready to slam the door in his face.

"Hold it," he said, shoving his foot in the doorstep. "You are Lilly Cooper, right?"

She barely nodded.

"You can talk to me now, or I can call the detective to re-open the case." He held up his cell phone. "I know who to call. I'm retired from the force. Now which shall it be?"

She glared at him defiantly. "I'm not going to let you in the house."

"I don't have to come in. We can talk here." Putting his phone back in his pocket, he pulled out a small notepad and pen. "Now Mrs. Cooper, I just need to ask you a few questions." He flipped to a page. "Where were you on the day of the storm?"

She shrugged and scowled. "Now, how am I supposed to know, just whip that date out of my memory bank?"

"Perhaps I can help jog your memory? The really big storm a year ago. You remember that?"

"Oh, the one that downed power lines and caused a lot of destruction… who can forget that?"

"Well, Mrs. Cooper, if you would just remember that storm, I'd like to get more specific information on where you were and what you were doing." Steve looked up, waiting.

"I suppose I was here, waiting out the storm like a lot of people."

"I get that, but were you out at any time that day, perhaps earlier, before it got really bad?"

She looked at him, but didn't answer.

Steve pressed her, "Mrs. Cooper, do you know someone named Gary?"

"Gary?"

"Yes, Gary. Who drives a taxi."

She felt a shiver run up her spine as realization slowly dawned on her. Still, she shook her head. "I'm afraid I don't know who you are talking about."

"Let me refresh your memory. The day of the storm, Gary, the taxi driver, was found dead outside, right in front of your home."

"The police have already questioned me. Why are you here?"

"I'm hired by the insurance company. You see, his life insurance policy covered death due to natural and accidental causes… but there was an exclusion clause."

"I don't understand…"

"According to the exclusion clause, we withhold payment in the case of a homicide."

He pulled out his card and handed it to her. "Mrs. Cooper, if you happen to remember anything, just give me a call. My phone number and email are both on the card. Anytime. You call me, okay?"

She nodded, afraid to speak, fearing the growing weakness in her voice would betray her this time. He withdrew his foot as she closed her door. She pressed her back against it, partly to hold it in place and partly to steady herself. Shaking slightly, she walked back to the kitchen and started the coffee.

She sat at the counter with her fresh cup, nursing the warm mug, her mind going back to that day. She had repelled all thoughts of what happened and, as time went on, it became easier to forget, to pretend that it had never taken place. Gary, so that was his name. She had never asked him.

Early on, Lilly had worried about the incident. She had convinced herself that it was an accident and blamed it on the weather. At that time, storm-related incidents were happening all over the city. No one had witnessed anything or come forth with any accusations. She simply assumed that they had forgotten about it, closing the book on it in the craziness that happened during and in the aftermath of the storm.

Now it had come back to haunt her after all this time. Lilly couldn't believe it. It was almost a year ago and they *hadn't* forgotten. Lilly forced herself to stay calm, to think. What if they didn't believe her this time? She repeated her thoughts, *There were no witnesses. It was just an accident.*

Steve knew something was off with Lilly Cooper. He didn't know exactly what yet. The operative word was *yet*. So it was just a matter of time until he got to the truth of the matter. Catching her off guard, when she least expected it.

He was a patient man. People get careless. They get forgetful. Or people get impatient. Or scared. They trip up somehow, they always do. They think they are smart, smarter than anyone out there.

Chapter 31

GIGI

GIGI TURNED HER HEAD, NUZZLING his cheek as she whispered, "Good night."

He still had his eyes closed, but a grin spread across his face. "No more nightmares, right?"

"Nope… nothing since that awful accident."

Reaching to pull her closer, Rex opened his eyes, showing the love in them, gazing at her face as if to etch it in his mind forever. "Gigi…"

Gigi smiled and moved closer, resting her head partially on his pillow.

His finger gently traced the curves of her upper lip to the edge, and around to her bottom. He murmured, "I love you" before planting a tender, sweet kiss on her lips.

BOOK 2 OF THE ALTERATIONS TRILOGY

GAME CHANGER

JANE SUEN

Chapter 1

DR. KITE

One year, three months and two days after the fire destroyed Dr. Kite's warehouse.

HER VOICE REACHED HIS EARS before he saw her. She was speaking, the words punctuated by soft laughter. What drew him closer, full of curiosity? Was it her tone, pleasant but firm? Perhaps he sensed it—her vitality, freshness, and energy. Before he realized it, he had walked down the grocery aisle to her sample meal kiosk.

She had an audience, watching as she dipped her spoon in a pot of chili simmering on an electric burner and divvied small portions into bite-sized paper cups on the counter. The finishing touch, a tiny plastic spoon, decorated each cup.

He stayed beyond the edge of the crowd, watching as she continued to talk, all the while doling out the samples. He was right about her. Young. Early twenties. Her long hair swept back in a ponytail.

She must have felt him staring at her as she held up a

sample of chili, scanning the crowd for volunteers willing to try it. Suddenly, she looked straight at him, her beautiful blue eyes innocent and wide.

He met her gaze before casting his eyes down. He looked at his rumpled pants, still full of creases from the day before, and the worn brown belt with the dull buckle at his waist, his crinkled, blue cotton shirt barely tucked in. Disgusted with himself, he quietly retreated, cursing his appearance, wishing he could change her first impression of him.

Chapter 2

ELLEN

WHEN ELLEN MISSED HER PERIOD, she dismissed it. *It's all this stress and trauma*, she thought. Sure, she had experienced irregularities in the past when her weight yo-yoed. She had chalked it up to another one and never gave it another thought. But, one month later, when her period didn't return, she couldn't help worrying. A suppressed memory surfaced of the day when she stepped into the little shop, the one with the Alterations sign. She stiffened, thinking, *What if the microchip has something to do with this?*

After work on Friday, she stopped at a drugstore. Overwhelmed by the choices available, she had no idea which one was better. She finally grabbed two pregnancy test kits and bought both, a pee-on-a-stick and a digital test kit.

Ellen waited until Saturday morning when she could take her time and not rush it. Waking up, she took the kits to the bathroom. She sat on the toilet lid, holding the first box in her hand, turning it over, rotating the sides to read each word. Tearing off the end tabs, Ellen pulled out the kit and the pregnancy test instruction. She unfolded the slip of paper, flattening and smoothing the creases on her lap. It had pictures explaining the results. A single line meant negative; double lines meant a positive test.

She held the test stick with care, pinching the handle end with two fingers. *Let's get this over with*, she prodded herself. She bent over the open toilet, slowly releasing the first stream of morning urine. She shoved the stick in its path, midstream.

Ellen averted her eyes from the stick. She resisted the urge to stare at it on the counter, focusing instead on the nearby LED alarm clock. She cursed, wishing she had a watch with a moving second hand, as she waited for the red numbers to change. Time appeared to stand still meanwhile her emotions were churning inside her. *What if there's something wrong with the display?*

Finally, when the results were ready, she looked. She bent closer, peering at the double lines. "Oh my God!" gasped Ellen, her mouth dropping open.

She blinked. Thoughts swirled in her head. How can this be? Me, a mother? I lost weight, but I'm gaining something else—a baby!

Ellen reached for the digital pregnancy test. Ripping open the package, she removed the test strip from the wrapper and peed on the absorbent tip. This time she set the timer on her cell phone and watched the countdown, waiting until one word appeared on the screen—*Pregnant.*

Chapter 3
DR. KITE

THE SOUND OF THE WAVES soothed him. An endless loop of incoming water crashing on the shore, retreating from the sand, rolling back in the ocean, leaving frothy bubbles in its path.

He closed his eyes behind the dark sunglasses. He lay on the sand, a towel beneath him, in a secluded area on the beach. He was safe here, far away from the busy madness of the city. Here, he'd recoup.

Kite ceased to care about his appearance after the warehouse fire took away all he had worked so hard to build—the microchips and experimental data. The fire also took away his dark secrets, hidden from plain view—the evidence of experiments gone bad, unknowing human subjects picked up by the taxis trawling the city streets from the previous night, later implanted with his microchips. Everything. Gone.

He left the city, escaping to the coast, to this small town. He no longer cared about himself, or anything, for that matter. Having been raised by strict parents, Kite had agonized over the loss. He had disappointed them, let them down after all they had sacrificed for him. A total failure.

He had applied a thin layer of sunscreen. Under the powerful rays, the sunscreen softened and melted, blending with his sweat and burning his eyes. Picking up the towel, he hastily wiped the cloth across his damp brow.

His dreams of fame and fortune crushed, he'd retreated to this hideaway to lick his wounds. And lick he did, letting himself go in the process. He knew he looked terrible, but he hadn't cared—until today.

Chapter 4
GIGI

THE BREEZE RUSTLED THE LEAVES on the trees. Gigi felt a slight caress, a light touch. Standing on the porch, Gigi took in the beauty of the land—the vast expanse, the faraway mountains, majestic and dignified, capped with snow.

She had Rex to thank. He brought her here, away from the city, where time seemed to stand still. The world beyond ceased to exist.

The sound of an ax splitting wood interrupted her thoughts. Methodical, rhythmic, like background noise. Subtle, not intrusive. She turned toward the back of the cabin, walking the worn path.

"Rex!" she shouted above the sound of the chopping, adding an urgency in her voice as her steps quickened.

As she rounded the corner, Rex came into view, dressed in a plaid shirt, jeans, and work gloves. Her heart raced as she laid her eyes on him. *Her man.*

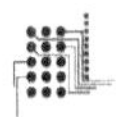

It had been three months, and two days since the morning she woke up next to Rex. The day their relationship took a new turn. It had started like any other day. He'd caught her by surprise. Okay, that part was romantic. They were having breakfast. She had picked up the napkin to wipe her mouth, and something fell out, making a soft noise as it flickered on the floor, brushing her foot before landing. She had stooped down to pick it up, and there they were—the two tickets.

Before she had a chance to say anything, Rex knelt down beside her. He was all solemn and serious. Holding her hand, he asked her to go away with him on this trip.

It seemed like Gigi had known him forever. They had been best friends for years, and roommates. Countless times they had helped each other out. She had cried on his shoulder and he'd always been there to comfort her. They had both dated other people, and boyfriends and girlfriends came and went. They stayed together as friends through thick and thin, sharing laughter and tears.

Gigi had looked at Rex, her eyes moist. "Do you remember when I had the nightmares?"

Rex nodded. "But the nightmares are gone now. You're safe."

During the ordeal with her illness, the nightmares that haunted her, the crash that came close to taking her life, Gigi had turned to Rex. Afterward, they became lovers.

But he wasn't done yet. He had another surprise for Gigi. He handed her an envelope.

"What's this?" said Gigi as she opened it, pulling out the reservation to the place he had rented. The brochure depicted enticing pictures of the mountains, a cabin with a creek running beside it, wild animals, and a spectacular sunrise. She could almost feel the breeze, suck in the crisp, clean air, see the wildlife, hear the trickle of water in the babbling brook. She squealed, excitement shining in her eyes. "I feel like I won the lottery!"

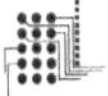

At last, they were here. All ten delicious days in their paradise, their piece of heaven. This place was indescribably beautiful, more than the photos had promised.

As she strode toward Rex, Gigi made a mental note to tell him how much she loved it here, with him. Could it be any more perfect? She was grateful. "Rex," she shouted, as she got closer to him.

He looked up, a smile spreading to his eyes.

"There's a message in the inbox." Stopping, she added, "I think you'll want to see it."

Chapter 5
GIGI

REX PUT THE AX DOWN on the ground, turning the blade away. He faced Gigi, arms outstretched, a boyish grin on his face. "Come here, where's my morning hug?"

"Who are you, Paul Bunyan?"

He threw back his head, laughing heartily, as the wind gently blew his shoulder-length locks. "I'll show you," he said, giving a swagger and throwing her his best charming smile.

She wasn't averse to his appeal, his awkward charm, irresistible and goofy. Gigi grinned, a bit out of breath as she approached, angling her body as she sought the hug.

"Hi, beautiful!" he said, wrapping his arms around her.

"You're up early."

"Hmm, you know what's the best thing in the morning next to coffee?"

"Me!"

Rex pretended to be bewildered, as boisterous laughter escaped his lips.

"Well." Gigi pouted, then blew him a kiss. "That's all you're going to get." She threw him a wink, gave an exaggerated shrug of her shoulders, and turned to leave.

In a few bounds, Rex reached her, wrapping his arms around her again, pulling her back. "Oh no, you don't! I'm not going to let you go so easily."

Turning her head and pushing his arms away in a playful shove, Gigi giggled. "Who says I'm an easy catch!"

"You are the best catch of all, and I've been fishing for a long time," whispered Rex as he buried his face in her thick, luxurious hair, inhaling the fresh scent of her lavender shampoo and a whiff of gardenia.

Gigi gave a wriggle and tugged at his arm, but she was held in a firm embrace. "Let me go."

"I'll never let you go," said Rex. His voice turned serious as he whispered, "You know this."

"I like it," said Gigi.

"Like what?"

"The way you are, everything about you."

"Huh—"

"I like you." Gigi reached to pull his head closer as she looked into his eyes and pressed her lips to his. "And I love you."

"Forever and ever?"

"And you?" she said, before pulling back to search his face. She wanted to hear his response. "And do you promise to love me always?"

"As long as we both shall live." He slipped one hand down her side, reaching to take hers, pulling her toward a large log. "My lady, please sit."

"My lord," she breathed out as she daintily stepped around the log and found a place to sit.

Rex scooted next to her, sitting close enough to feel the shiver run through her body. Picking up the jacket he'd thrown across the log, he draped it across her shoulders.

They sat in silence, enjoying the scenery.

"Look how beautiful this place is. It's God's country," said Rex, nudging Gigi.

"So pristine, untouched."

"Breathtaking."

"You know what the best part is? I'm here to enjoy it with you."

"It wouldn't be the same without you," said Rex. He sat there, content. He'd be happy to stay for more than ten days, for as long as they could.

"You know, Rex?"

"What Gigi?"

"All the stuff, the bad stuff happening to me over a year ago . . ." She paused, frowning as her eyes narrowed, "I tried to block it out and forget it. It's like, sometimes I wonder if it even happened."

"It's all in the past," said Rex, turning to plant a soothing kiss on her forehead. "You don't have to relive those nightmares anymore. Forget it."

"But something good came out of it," Gigi reminded him. "If we hadn't gone through it all together, we probably wouldn't be here now." She moved her hand, touching his thumb, wrapping her fingers around it.

He pulled his thumb back. He laughed as Gigi kept her

grip on it, starting a playful tug-of-war, back and forth.

"We've had some tough times, but you are a survivor. Remember this." Rex clasped her chin with his free hand, raising her upturned face to his before planting a kiss on her trembling lips.

"Don't stop."

He kissed her until he felt the trembling subside. He turned his face, kissing the concave roundness of her palm, moving his attention to her slender fingers and dainty wrist.

"Rex, do you know how many bones are in our hands?"

"No clue."

"I looked it up once, about twenty-seven." She stretched her hands out.

He pressed her hand, gently rubbing it.

Gigi grabbed his wrist, playfully running her slim fingers down the length of his palm.

"Ooh, it tickles."

"I thought so," she said, laughing. "I can think of some other places to tickle . . ."

Gigi gave way to this playfulness, choosing not to mention the email again, preferring not to let anything ruin this happy moment as she wriggled and poked her finger in the ticklish parts of his sides.

Chapter 6
DR. KITE

HOW MANY MONTHS HAD IT been since the fire destroyed his warehouse? More than fifteen months—a year and three months and two days plus.

Defeated, he'd left the city. For a long time, he stayed in isolation, imprisoning himself in his cheap apartment in the coastal town. As the weeks turned into months, he descended into despair mixed with a plentiful dose of self-pity.

The times he went out, he'd walk to the grocery store. A quick trip a couple of blocks away. Once there, he'd grab the items and throw them in the cart, following the same routine and route in the store. He barely looked up to see where he was going, or to view who was shopping or to dawdle and check out any new items.

Today was different. Kite had a secret agenda and headed straight to the food sample kiosk where he had watched *her* the other day, the one with the baby-blue eyes luring customers to her samples. She had sure lured him.

Today, little paper cups filled with cheesecake dotted the counter.

He reached out, hiding his disappointment at the sight of the matronly woman with old-fashioned glasses perched on her nose. He grabbed the cup closest to him. He feigned interest, conjuring the smooth, rich taste of the heavy cream, savoring each bite. Well, in this case, one bite.

He crushed the bottom of the thin paper cup, fingers tapping as his head tilted back, mouth opening to receive the piece of cake.

"Sir! Would you like to try our newest flavor of cheesecake?"

Stopping in mid-air, he said, "I've got it."

"No, sir, what you got was last year's flavor—strawberry cheesecake," said the woman, vehemently shaking her head. "You have to try the new flavor, blackberry swirl cheesecake." She pointed to a row of cups.

"Huh?" he managed as he shook the morsel in his mouth.

She smiled as she handed him another one. "You're going to like this."

He grabbed it and plopped in the second piece of cake, grimacing at the sugary overload and sudden dryness in his mouth. "You got anything to drink?"

Twisting the cap off of a bottled drink, she filled another paper cup. "Fizzy tangerine is all I've got."

He drank it in a quick gulp and tossed the cup in the waste can full of other paper cups. He snatched a napkin from a caddy filled with spoons and forks to wipe his face. He took another look at the woman, thinking, *too bad it's not her.*

"You like it?"

He managed a weak smile. "Do you do this every day?"

"Me? Naw, two times a week, occasionally three. I'm here Mondays and Wednesdays."

"I was here yesterday, but I saw another girl. Oh, um . . . what was her name?"

"Tiffany. She's our new girl here. Tuesdays and Fridays."

"So the two of you do this?"

"We had another person, but she'd quit, so they hired Tiffany."

He hid his glee behind his smile as he turned to leave. *Two more days until Friday.*

Chapter 7

LILLY

THE MUSIC BLASTING FROM THE alarm clock abruptly woke her. Lilly groaned and settled back under the covers, at first ignoring the sound. Her hand slammed down on the snooze button; the room stilled again.

She lay on the pillow, letting her thoughts wander. She wasn't one to run away from anything. Not even during a personal crisis like a divorce. She took it on like a thankless job, distasteful but necessary, something to get over as quickly as possible. Today she had a decision to make.

Rolling on her side, she glimpsed the framed photo on the table next to her bed. An exclusive piece of real estate, as some would say. Looking at it for the umpteenth time, Lilly saw herself, the little girl standing between her parents, wearing the one well-worn dress she had which her mother insisted she put on. Her hair was scraggly, a long time between haircuts. But the look of the little girl's face said it all. Defiant, tough. Bearing the scars of her short life.

"That's my girl," she said, looking at the photo. The

child she was. Captured on film. Lilly never had an easy life; everything she'd ever wanted she worked hard to get. Her father wished for a boy and showed his disappointment when she burst out into the world. He even wanted to name her Sam or some less-feminine variation of Samantha. But his wife wouldn't hear of it. She insisted on naming her baby. For once, she had her way.

She recalled the story her mother told about her birth certificate. The nurse in the hospital had asked her mother for the baby's name as she filled out the form for the birth certificate. Her mother said, "Lily," but when the nurse asked to confirm this, her mother, exhausted and weakened from the delivery, struggled to reply, "You know, it rhymes with Billy." So the nurse wrote down "Lilly" on the form next to her name.

Growing up, her father treated her like a boy—the boy he never had. She wanted to please him, and even dressed up as a boy and acted like a tomboy. He wasn't cruel to her, but he was severe, keeping a belt handy, which he had no qualms about using. Ever mindful of it, Lilly acted out her rebelliousness when she was with friends, but toned it down when she came home. She learned how to survive, avoiding a beating whenever she could.

Chapter 8
ELLEN

ELLEN TAPPED THE TIPS OF her crimson, manicured nails on the notepad as she scrutinized the schedule, seeing it was tight but workable. She smiled and looked a short distance across the room to the closed door of her boss's office—her *new* boss, Andrew Capstone. *Her dream job.* After years of working for the same company, she finally got the nerve to look elsewhere.

She told herself she had an extra mouth to feed now, to care for a baby. Somehow, this gave her the strength she never had before, the final push to leave the place where she'd been working in the administrative pool.

The transformation shocked even her. She became a tigress in a man's world, competing for the lofty position she longed to have.

When she submitted her resume for the executive assistant to the director position at dEsign+, it wasn't an empty title. It had the salary to match. *Her* job, she fiercely reminded herself the day they called her to set up the interview. She bought a new outfit and had her hair and nails done.

Ellen strode into the interview room like a queen, like she owned the place, like she already had the position. And she knew, instantly and without a doubt, she had their attention and a chance at her dream job.

At the end of the interview, the director rushed up to shake her hand. She rewarded him with a cool and confident smile before she walked out.

Later in the day, the phone rang. The woman from HR said, "We'd like to offer you the job." She quoted the stated salary plus a bonus of 10 percent.

Ellen was elated, momentarily at a loss for words at the offer and a generous bonus above the industry average.

"Do you accept?"

"Yes. When do I start?"

"You can negotiate the date with your new boss, Andrew Capstone."

New boss. The words thrilled her.

He called her unexpectedly later that afternoon to congratulate her. They negotiated a good starting date. She was ready to go now but didn't say it. He wanted her sooner than later. She pushed for a later date with the excuse that she needed to take some time to wrap up the work she was doing, to leave on a good note. They agreed on the first of the following month—a Monday—which was fifteen days away.

She submitted an adequate notice to her company, giving the date of resignation. She proceeded to get herself ready for the new job in the meantime, meeting with Mr. Capstone next week to go over some preliminary items.

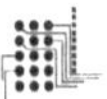

They met at the cafe across the street from the office. He had insisted on taking Ellen out to lunch to discuss the job.

"Looking forward to you coming on board, Ellen."

"Mr. Capstone," she blurted out, but he waved his hand.

"Call me Andy," he said.

Sitting next to him, Ellen had a chance to observe him close up. He appeared to be younger than she thought. She scrutinized him discreetly, taking an extra few seconds to study his face. She liked a man with salt and pepper hair—a full head of hair, no less. He looked distinguished. He appeared impeccably dressed, comfortable even in a shirt and tie.

"We've had a slew of executive assistants in the past few months who haven't worked out, and I'm hoping you'll be the one to stay."

Ellen gulped. Fidgeting in her seat, taking a sip of water, she bought some time to think. "I have no intention of leaving any time soon."

He laughed. "I'm pulling your leg. The prior occupant of your office went on maternity leave." He paused, leaning closer. "So we got temps from the agency, and they sent a different girl each week."

"Oh," Ellen said, letting out a sigh of relief. "I can't imagine how crazy it must have been."

"We managed somehow, but I'm so glad things will be going back to normal now that you're here."

Ellen raised her eyebrow. "What about the girl, the one on maternity leave . . . isn't she coming back?"

"She changed her mind after the baby. You got her job, but not exactly."

"What do you mean?"

"We upscaled it and expanded the role."

"Sir, I'll do my best," she managed to say with a brave smile, wondering if she'd have a mess to clean up.

"I'm sure you'll have a lot of questions. Speak up. I won't bite."

"I do have a question. I have a baby—well, she's a few months old now. My mother helps take care of her while I'm working." She exhaled and tucked her hair back. "Would you expect me to work late?"

He looked at her, taking time to assimilate the new information before he answered. "I may at times, depending on our deadlines. Would it be a problem?"

She thought it over. "My baby comes first. But if you need me to stay late, I'll need a heads-up and enough time to make arrangements."

"I thought your mother is taking care of her?"

"Well yes, but it's presumptive and unfair to expect her to drop everything in her life and revolve her schedule around me."

"Quite right."

"She has her own life, and I can't blame her."

"When the time comes, we'll work it out."

"Thanks," she said, relieved this was going well.

After lunch, they went back to the company for a quick tour. Ellen's new office was catty-corner from the enormous corner room of her boss. Hers was small, but enough.

When Ellen arrived on the first day, a shiny new plate on her door bore her name and title emblazoned on copper: Ellen Fulbright, Executive Assistant to the Director. It caught her attention. She touched it with her fingertip, feeling the solid substance, admiring it.

With her hand on the doorknob, Ellen paused for a moment. Opening the door, a huge bouquet of fresh flowers on her desk greeted her. The delicate scent, the pastel colors cast in the sea of slender green stalks, delighted her senses.

She pressed her back to the closed door, soaking it in as she surveyed the scene. Someone had cleaned the desk and placed new office supplies beside the computer—a pen holder, file caddy, portfolio, stack of paper pads, shiny pens, pencils, clips. Pulling out the top drawer of her desk, she saw the smaller items in an organizer. A first aid kit tucked in the back of her drawer caught her attention. "Oh." She let out a sigh as her lips parted in a smile.

Chapter 9
GIGI

She peered in the mirror. No trace of lines around her eyes. Funny how her face was still flawless with no signs of aging. Other women spent fortunes on creams or potions to turn back Father Time, even for a few hours. Others went under the knife for a more lasting effect. She used to laugh at how much money they threw away, chasing after one promise or another. Gigi would have none of it; she didn't need to.

Gigi gently tugged at her skin, stretching it, releasing it, and then watching as it relaxed back to its original position. What she feared hadn't happened—her first line. But her relief now lacked the satisfying pretentiousness she exhibited before, although she still laughed it off, saying she had good genes.

As her friends despaired over each new wrinkle, she had kept her thoughts quietly to herself. But it didn't erase the fact she was insensitive to her friends' fears of aging.

But, after surviving the car accident, something changed

inside her. Before, she had focused on her appearance—a perfect appearance. Afterward, it didn't seem to matter as much. She moved beyond it, past the fixation on the superficial part of her, her flawless skin and great beauty, shifting to the inner part of her being. Gigi sought out happiness from other things in life, things that mattered.

The car accident. She tried not to think of it, not to relive it. It still terrified her, and she made a considerable effort to avoid that spot on the road, finding detours, taking other routes instead.

In an instant, her life almost snatched away. She thought about what she would have left behind, the people she loved, memories to be created. A life not lived. She would have regretted that.

Gigi was grateful, for she had a second chance now, and she was determined to live her life fully, to love like she never loved before, to live each day like the gift it was. It wasn't too late.

Chapter 10
DR. KITE

THE TREK TO THE GROCERY store became a scheduled event on Kite's calendar. He marked it in red ink, circling the days Tiffany would be working at the sample meal kiosk. It became a habit, close to an obsession. Somehow it triggered a change in him, energized him, gave him something to look forward to, like a kid looks forward to birthdays, but on a smaller scale. Her schedule became his.

He became more aware of his appearance, how unattended it had become. On a trip to the grocery store, he picked up mouthwash, toothpaste, deodorant, shampoo, shaving cream, a pack of disposable razor cartridges, and plenty of soap.

He made changes. Small, but significant. First, he got a haircut; later he shaved off his scraggly beard. Bit by bit, Kite's life returned as layer upon layer of disarray and neglect was peeled away, replaced with attention and freshness.

The transformation in his appearance spilled over to his habits. He had slacked off on his laundry, throwing a worn shirt and pants over his unwashed body. Now he showered more often and regularly, on a daily basis. His clothes went in the washer after being worn once, instead of strewn all over the floor to be re-worn, sometimes two or three times as he lost track of how many times he'd worn a piece of clothing before it got washed.

Each time he went back to see Tiffany, he peeled off another layer. He became lighter, cleaner, less constrained. His confidence gradually returned.

They established this communication, this routine, as the weeks went by. Tiffany changed too, gradually warming up, paying him compliments when his transformations became a source of pride in his behavior.

The words they exchanged now became less formal, more playful, correlating with his transformation, going way beyond the initial conversation they had, when she'd say, "Hello, sir, would you like to try a sample today?"

"What? You're back. Weren't you here earlier this week on Tuesday and the weeks before that?" Tiffany would say.

"Your menus change each time. I hate to miss one." He'd smile. "Besides, it's become a habit, twice a week, you know."

She'd smile back.

"Hmm," he'd say, stepping closer to look. "What do we have here?"

"Well, today we have savory black-eyed peas."

"Oh, I'll try it," he'd say, reaching for a sample, picking up the miniature spoon from the caddy and digging into the food.

She'd fix her eyes upon him as he ate. She couldn't say what kept her fascinated. To see if he'd enjoy each mouthful, each taste, each texture, or spit it out, disposing the pre-chewed food on a napkin? One thing she knew for sure; he'd give her an honest response.

He'd always finish if the taste test survived beyond the first bite. When done, he'd lick the tiny spoon, carefully placing the spoon inside the cup, dunking it into the trash can nearby. He'd respond to her. A smile or a nod, if it passed. He didn't mince words if it didn't.

She grew to understand his mannerisms, to interpret his pleasure or displeasure without him ever having to say much.

After weeks of variations of the same talk about food, food, and more food, their conversation wandered off the grid. They talked about other things, allowing more hints each time, of their lives, hopes, dreams, and even fears.

Each morsel or tidbit she divulged, shared, gave freely, later became fodder for Kite to relish, to turn over and over, to savor and stretch out until the next encounter.

Kite figured that she didn't realize how much he had changed until, one day, when he spoke to her, when he looked, acted, and had become another person.

Only then did he learn her full name. Tiffany Grant. *Oh yeah, I've got your name. Now, to get your number.*

Chapter 11

ELLEN

THE FIRST DAY PASSED IN a flash. Ellen threw herself into her new job, learning as much as she could. She snapped a picture of her office, the flowers in full bloom, to show her mom.

They celebrated after work. Ellen took her parents out for dinner to the new restaurant she wanted to try. She got a sitter for Angie, someone who came with references, a certification, and first aid training. If this worked out, she'd hire her during the week, a day or two, to give her mom a break.

Ellen's thoughts never strayed far from her baby. Angie was her world now, her whole world.

"Mom, how was Angie today?"

"Angie likes the new picture book you got her. We read it together, and she picks up the words and associations."

"She's learning fast."

"Angie pointed to the picture of the dog today. Said 'dada.'"

"Darn, I missed it!" said Ellen, as a pang of guilt flickered. Being a single mom had its moments, but this sucked, not being able to stay at home with her baby.

"There'll be many more."

"She's a smart one," said Ellen. She was eager to wrap up the dinner and get home.

They ordered dessert to go, a luscious, dark-and-white cake with matching frosting over each half—rich caramel topping drizzled over one side, marshmallows topping the dark chocolate frosting on the other, with a light dusting of crushed nuts over it all.

At the front entrance of her home, she handed the dessert box to her mom and unlocked the door, preparing to greet the babysitter.

"We're home!" said Ellen, shouting over the noise blasting from the TV.

The babysitter was sitting in front of the TV, her feet propped on the table, chips spilling out from an opened bag next to a can of soda. "Oh, hi," she said, her mouth crammed full of chips, hastily chewing. "You're home early. I wasn't expecting you yet."

Ellen laughed. "Angie's in bed?"

"Yeah, she's sleeping," she said. "I gave her a bath and tucked her in." Wiping her greasy fingers on her jeans, she got up, glancing down at the bag of chips.

"You can have them."

"I'm outta here."

"I'll bill pay your account," said Ellen as the babysitter dashed out, headed to her car.

Chapter 12

LILLY

SHE STOOD IN THE MIDDLE of the circle, surrounded by women. Pivoting slowly, Lilly looked around, locking eyes with each in a silent greeting. Altogether, an even dozen. An exclusive group. With a satisfied nod, she spoke.

"Welcome to this retreat, a quiet sanctuary away from the rest of the world." She paused to give a brief smile. "My name is Lilly Cooper, and your host for the next two weeks. I know some of you have made a sacrifice to be here, to take this next step in your life. But like anything you endeavor, the outcome is what you put in. I'm here to give you the means. You have to do the rest."

A murmur went around the group, accompanied by a few nods.

"First, a few ground rules. One, turn off electronics. We want you to focus your attention here and do the program. Two, no photos are allowed. Three, you will have to sign a nondisclosure agreement." She paused. "If you don't agree, speak up now."

A hand went up. A thirty-something blonde spoke. "Lilly, what if there's an emergency at home, and someone needs to get hold of you?"

"What's your name?"

"Hanna."

"We have a number for people outside to call. It's on the agreement."

"So they can call in, and we can talk to them?"

"Yes, if it's an emergency."

Hanna sighed in relief. "I read your preliminary guidance in the preparation before coming here. I didn't see a phone number. So we give out this number to people back home before we start?"

"Yes, as soon as you sign the agreement," said Lilly, pointing to a table with two neat piles of papers and a dozen pens laid out. A girl sat behind it. "Naomi will help you out and show you to your rooms. You'll get three meals a day. If you have any dietary restrictions or allergies, please fill out the other form."

A mousy brunette with glasses raised her hand. "I have a question about our rooms. Are we sharing and with whom?" Twisting her head to seek support from the other women, she asked, "I don't know anyone here. How are you going to decide our roommate situation?"

Lilly nodded to Naomi.

Naomi slid out from behind the table. She carried a glass bowl with folded pieces of paper. All eyes focused on her. "I have twelve slips of paper. Each of you will draw a piece of paper from this bowl. On it will be a number from one to twelve." She moved to the middle of the circle. "I'll call out the number one. Whoever has it will call out another number from seven to twelve. The person with that number will be her roommate. I'll repeat this process calling out numbers two through six."

An older woman with streaks of gray in her hair spoke up. "So if you get a number greater than six you don't get to choose?"

"That's right," said Naomi. She raised the glass bowl higher for all to see. A hushed silence settled over the room. "Now, who wants to be the first one to draw?"

Immediately three hands were raised.

"Take one step forward, please," said Naomi. "Each of you will tell the group why you want to be the first. Make it short. We'll go clockwise." She nodded to one woman. "You're first."

"Hi, I'm Geraldine. I'd like to get lucky for once." She didn't elaborate.

A tall woman was next. "I'm Katherine; you can call me Katy." She managed a feeble smile. "This would make my day. By golly, I need it."

The last hand up belonged to the mousy brunette. "I asked the question about the roommates. I deserve to be the first."

Lilly glanced at her watch. "Let's take a vote on who goes first now. You can't vote for yourself. Then we'll draw to decide your rooms. You'll have two hours to unpack and get settled. Be sure to dress comfortably. We'll meet back here for lunch. "

Chapter 13
GIGI

SHE HEARD THE KNOCK ON the front door. She glanced at Rex, still asleep after their late night rousing and lovemaking. Grabbing a T-shirt, she struggled to pull it over her head. Shoving her legs into her jeans, Gigi cursed at the tightness. "Be right there!" she shouted.

Limping as she stumbled, pulling and snapping her pants in place, she hurried to the door. "Who is it?"

"I have a delivery," a male voice replied.

She opened the door a crack, peeking past the taut door chain at the man who stood outside, package in his hand. "I'm not expecting anything. You sure you have the right address?"

"Here," he said, pointing to her name and address on the label.

"What's this?"

"You'll have to sign for it."

Gigi peered at the box, raising her eyebrows at the guy holding it. "Good God, you came all the way out here to the middle of nowhere?" She muttered, repeating to herself. "I'm not expecting this. What could it be?"

"Ma'am, sign here please," he spoke with the measured ease and politeness of someone who's uttered the same words before, many times.

She stared at him, noticing he was barely a man, the boyishness of his face at odds with the starched severity of his uniform. Gigi opened the door, stepped out, and grabbed his pen, scribbling her name. "All done," she said, giving it back to him.

"Thank you," he said, rewarding her with a shy smile, his eyes flickering over her shoulder partly exposed by the T-shirt pulled low, pressing tightly over her breast.

She caught his glimpse and impulsively pushed out her chest, taunting him to have another look. Old habits die hard.

He cleared his throat, moving his eyes away, but not before sneaking another glance.

Bored already with this game, she snatched the box, seeing the red-stamped words, "Handle with care." As he turned around to leave, she uttered a "thank you" to his departing back.

Setting it carefully on the kitchen table, Gigi went to get scissors from the drawer, thinking, *I wonder what's inside.*

Chapter 14
DR. KITE

ONE DAY, ON WHAT STARTED off as another routine sampling, he grew alarmed when she seemed woozy and unsteady. "Tiffany, you're not your usual self. What's going on? How can I help?"

"I'm not asking for help."

"No, but *I'm* asking," he said firmly.

Kite sprung into action, stepping around the kiosk to reach Tiffany as she braced herself, one hand gripping the edge of the counter. An employee working in the fresh produce section witnessed this and rushed over, offering her help.

"Get the manager," shouted Kite.

"Is she all right?"

"The manager. Now!"

As she hurried off, he turned his attention back to Tiffany. He wrapped his arm around her shoulder, supporting her as she leaned slightly into him.

He whispered, "Tiffany, tell me what's wrong."

"I'm not feeling well."

"Are you sick?"

"I feel dizzy."

He grabbed a bottle of water from the display case behind her cart and gently lowered her with him to sit on the floor, stretching out his legs and holding her head against his chest. With a twist, he uncapped the drink and lowered it, pressing the rim to her lips.

"Here, drink this slowly."

She took a sip.

"We're going to take you to the doctor, find out what's wrong. Okay?"

She gave a slight nod as she swallowed another drink of water.

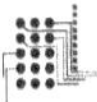

He took her to the nearest urgent care, accompanying her as the doctor checked her out.

The doctor asked her a series of questions, a history of her medical conditions, what medications she was taking, any other symptoms. With some reluctance, she eventually divulged she was on medication.

"This medication, how many times a day do you take it?" the doctor asked.

"I was taking it three times a day, with meals."

"Was?"

"I mean, but . . ."

"So what do you mean?"

Embarrassed, Tiffany sought support, her eyes pleading.

"Let's start over," said the doctor. "You're still taking this medication?"

She nodded.

"Three times a day?"

"Well, no." She shook her head.

"So how many times a day?"

"Sometimes once a day, or twice."

"So you're not taking this medicine according to the prescription?"

"No," mumbled Tiffany.

"Are you too busy, forgetting to take it?"

Tiffany looked back and forth, from the doctor to Kite. She shook her head in resignation.

"But why?"

"I, um, I wanted to save . . ." gulped Tiffany. "Save money."

The doctor gripped her arm. "Did you decrease your dosage to stretch it out because you can't afford it?"

"I had to," she whispered.

He sighed. "Now you understand the potential danger in not following the dosage."

Chapter 15

DR. KITE

He made sure Tiffany was settled in her home before he grabbed a microwave dinner and headed back to his place.

Splashing cold water on his face, he closed his eyes as it stung his cheeks. Holding his face in his palms, he cradled it. Sighing, he reached for the towel and wiped his face dry.

He sat in a straight-backed chair at the small table, the surface bare except for a cold beer and his tray of microwave dinner. He was still shaken up about the day, and a few things surprised him.

In his mind, he had built up this fantasy about Tiffany. He'd put her on a pedestal and worshipped at her throne twice each week, punctual like the Sunday service and Wednesday nights he remembered from his childhood. She became his savior, one of his own making, but still powerful, as his adoration of her transformed him, as nothing and no one had ever done before.

For years, he had existed in selfish depravity and ruthlessness, caring for no one, driven by his desire for immortality, to change the world—on his terms, at all costs. But when Kite lost it all, he descended into hell, plunging to its depths.

He wallowed in self-pity, ceased to care about anything after the fire burned the warehouse, microchips, computer, and data. And along with these, his inner spirit, his drive . . . perhaps even his blackened, tarred soul.

However recently something had stirred, like green sprouts poking up through the black soil, stirring his feelings for the first time.

Chapter 16
ELLEN

WAITING AT THE RED LIGHT, she reached for her travel mug tucked down in the holder beside the driver's seat. Glancing at the clock on her dashboard and the traffic, Ellen figured she'd be at least ten minutes early today, again. Although this new job meant she had farther to travel and needed to get up earlier, the longer drive also gave her more time to think. She ticked off the pluses of this new job like a mantra, repeating the words: "better job, more money, fancy title." All the hard work had paid off. She graduated to this hard-won position.

The cell phone rang as the dashboard screen announced the caller's identity. She pressed the button on her wheel to take the call. "Mom."

"Ellen, I forgot to mention this before you left."

"What?"

"You need to pick up diapers."

"No problem. I'll grab them on my way back. Anything else?"

"We could use more wipes too."

"Okay, Mom."

"What time will you be home?"

"Adding the grocery stop, hmm, I'm guessing around six or seven at the latest," said Ellen. "Will it be a problem?"

"No, tonight's okay, don't be too late."

"Thanks, Mom, you're the best."

Ellen ended the call and settled back in her seat, thinking she had a lot of responsibilities now. Her baby. A new job. Single mom. *She wanted to do it all, and now she'd gotten her wish.*

Chapter 17
GIGI

SHE SLIT A LINE DOWN the center of the box with the tip of the scissors, then threw it on the table and used her hands to rip it open, revealing a gift box and a white card inside. On the envelope, one word: "Gigi." She rubbed her finger across the paper, feeling the raised bump of the letters in her name and the thick, rich texture of the handmade paper.

She read the few words on the card and smiled. Rex. She couldn't help feeling a bit flattered, thinking that he shouldn't have taken the trouble to do this.

She held the gift box, relishing the moment a little longer before carefully untying the ribbon around it. Nestled inside was a case. A gasp escaped her lips as she opened it.

A heart, a ruby jewel necklace, surrounded by diamonds.

She looked toward the bedroom, smiling as she thought of Rex. They had all the time in the world.

Chapter 18

LILLY

LILLY SAT IN HER OFFICE, flipping through the forms, counting as she went along. All the women had signed. Touching the sleeve of her expensive business suit, she gave it a slight tug. After today's welcome and opening session, she would ditch it for something comfortable. But for now, she looked every bit a successful businesswoman.

She had put the past behind her, determined to carve out a new life after the nasty divorce. Initially, Lilly allowed herself some time to grieve, to console and feel sorry for herself. It hadn't been easy. She was at her weakest, having used up her energy reserves in the fight for her marriage— only to lose out at the end.

Lilly had fought her inner demons. She choked back the bitterness, the bile rising at those moments of anger. Most of all, she sought to salvage her wounded pride, lamenting the loss of love, the cruelty in which he cast her aside.

She jerked, hearing a knock on the door.

"Lilly, may I come in?"

"Wait a minute," said Lilly. She took the time to compose herself, to wipe the tears from her eyes, before calling out, "Come in."

Naomi poked her head around the door, beaming. "Lunch will be ready in twenty minutes."

"Good." Lilly nodded. "I'll see you there in fifteen."

As the door closed behind Naomi, Lilly opened her purse, searching for the key to the locked compartment. Retrieving it, she inserted the key in the drawer of her desk, the place she kept some files hidden. Lilly flipped back the tips of the file folders, scanning the names on the labels toward the end. The rise of her eyebrow signaled success as she snatched up the file.

Lilly took a deep breath before she opened the manila file folder. With her fingertip, she pushed the paper clip away from the pages, thumbing quickly until she found what she was looking for. She smiled before shutting the file, inserting it back into the drawer in alphabetical order with the name showing on the label. Tiffany.

Chapter 19
LILLY

She joined the buffet line, picking up a plate.

Lilly moved forward as her stomach growled. She took the tongs and dropped two scoops of mixed green salad on her plate, then picked out a sandwich, making a selection from several choices offered, before grabbing a plate with a small wedge of frosted cake. Oh, no sweets, Lilly reminded herself. She tossed her head, heading to the table with the slice in hand. She had cut out the desserts for the most part, but today she made an exception.

When lunch was over, Naomi shepherded the women back into the same room, the chairs now arranged in two rows. This time, Lilly sat behind the table with Naomi. After a nice meal, and the time to unpack and rest a bit, the women were at ease, chatting, getting to know each other better. Lilly nodded to Naomi.

The chime of a triangle got their attention. Lilly stood, walking in front of the table.

"Ladies, I trust you are fully alert and eager to get started."

Quite a few heads nodded, amidst a couple saying, "Yes."

"First, I'd like to welcome you again." Lilly looked around, making sure she had eye contact with each one. "I know many of you have made sacrifices to be here, to clear your schedule, to make arrangements, to be available for the next two weeks." She paused. "Let's remember this. You *wanted* to be here. You *chose* to be here."

The room was quiet. A discrete cough sounded, quickly muffled behind a covered hand.

Lilly continued. "You've all read the paperwork this morning with the details and what we'll be doing, and all of you signed it. There are fourteen days in this program, weekends included. You will be expected to participate every day."

A hand went up, the fingers impatiently waving, determined to catch her attention.

"Hanna, you have a question?"

"Are we going to be graded? I mean, if we work harder, is there some reward?"

"Would it make a difference, working harder?"

She shook her head. "I mean, is this like a class?"

Lilly suppressed the tiniest bit of irritation. "Not in the sense of traditional classes. As you progress through each mile marker, you'll have the self-satisfaction of having succeeded. But I caution you; we'll be watching how you achieve it."

"So how will we know what you'll be looking for?" Hanna persisted.

"There will be set instructions, and there will be

opportunities for you to be creative, to use all of your intellect and resources. Think outside the box."

"Umm," Hanna gulped. "It sounds like you're throwing us a challenge."

"Can I count on you?"

She nodded.

"Are you up for it?" Lilly asked her. Raising her voice, she directed her question again to the whole group. "Are you *all* up for it?"

"Yes," a chorus of voices responded.

"Again!"

This time, the reply was much louder.

Chapter 20

DR. KITE

HE AWOKE, KICKING THE SHEET with his feet. After his tossing and turning all night, the bed was a rumpled mess. He fumbled, reaching for his cell phone to check the time. Four o'clock in the morning. Sighing, he fell back on the pillow, willing sleep to return, but his eyes remained open.

He raised his hand, the one that had cradled Tiffany's head and touched her hair. Ah, what was the scent of her hair? He breathed in and out, trying to recapture the light fragrance. He closed his eyes to recreate the moment in a slow replay.

Inches from her face, he discovered she had a few fine lines, faint but discernible. Her forehead was smooth and noble, and her thick lashes lay on her cheeks like a feather fan, ready to flutter open, revealing her blue eyes. Her nose stood, pert and spunky.

Transfixed by the drop of water clinging to the edge of her lip from the water bottle, he dared not wipe it. He only stared, bent over her. His imagination ran wild. He wondered how many lips had kissed her.

A feeling of power and protectiveness stirred in him as he recognized her vulnerability. The realization sent a surge through him.

In the doctor's office, her revelations had disturbed him just as much as the doctor. It never occurred to him she could be poor and not be taking her meds.

In the early days, Kite had developed a prototype microchip to track medications, to ensure patients took them on time. His initial thoughts focused on the elderly, those with dementia, Alzheimer's, other brain disorders. However, later, he abandoned it for the more glamorous microchips, the ones more appealing to those seeking beauty, weight loss, and health.

Unable to sleep, Kite got up to pace the room, to think. That prototype . . . did he still have the plans somewhere? He had stored the other microchips in the warehouse and their files on the main computer there. But the medication prototype hadn't been kept there, he was sure of it. Fired up now, he opened his laptop on the desk, turning on the lamp.

Sitting and staring at the screen, Kite groaned. Dare he raise his hopes? He searched, his heart beating faster, scrolling quickly. In his paranoia, he had encrypted files and sometimes split them into several locations. Now he'd have to piece them together. As the minutes ticked by, he grew more determined. He was going to find them, no matter what. He had to do this and do this now. A renewed sense of urgency, of importance, took hold. Nothing could deter him at the moment. Tiffany's well-being might depend on it. On *him*.

Chapter 21
ELLEN

SHE TOOK ANOTHER LOOK AT the presentation, a last-minute check before the meeting this afternoon. A lot was on the line with this first project, this lucrative deal in the making—her new job, Andrew Capstone's trust in her.

"How did I miss it?" she gasped as her eyes caught a typo on the slide, after going over it the *nth* time. Exasperated, she marked the slide and updated the file, making a note to have it replaced in the folder and to alert the presenter. Not a huge error, but to her, it stuck out like a sore thumb.

Ellen glanced at the desk clock. Another hour would give her time to finish up and have a quick lunch in her office while copies were made and updated in all the meeting folders.

She'd be heading to the conference room well ahead of the scheduled meeting time.

She stopped by the bathroom to touch up, applying fresh lipstick and coaxing a few strands of hair back in place. She turned her body, observing it in the mirror, pleased at the way her new suit hugged the curvy outline of her body, accentuating it. She'd kept her weight down after the baby. Tugging the waistline of her size eight pants, she slipped two fingers inside the waistband easily. She felt the looseness, even after lunch. Good. Time for some new clothes, size six.

Ellen walked into the conference room forty-five minutes before 2:00 p.m. She made a visual check. The large wood conference table had been cleaned and polished, the shine and faint lemony smell telltale signs. Name cards were in place, along with meeting folders embossed with the company name on the cover, leather portfolios with writing pads, expensive pens with the company logo, water glasses, and small bowls filled with miniature chocolate bars, handmade by a world-famous chocolatier and express shipped here for the occasion.

The IT guys were quietly working on the opposite side of the room, testing to make sure things worked smoothly. They had installed state-of-the-art equipment Andy had purchased. One of the guys looked up as she walked in.

"Any problems?"

"We're doing the final checks now."

Ellen walked along the table and toward the tall, dark-haired guy. "I haven't met you before. What's your name?"

"Kevin."

"Pleased to meet you. I'm Ellen," she said as she reached out to shake his hand.

"Yes, ma'am."

"Kevin," she said, separating each syllable in his name. "Would you mind running through the presentation for me?"

He nodded, already loading it up.

She pulled back a chair, sitting down. After watching, she was pleased. "Thank you, Kevin." Now she'd leave it up to the presenters to do their job.

Andrew Capstone stuck his head in, his smile widening at the sight of Ellen. "All set?"

"Looks good, boss."

Chapter 22

GIGI

SHE SQUIRMED, SNUGGLING CLOSER TO Rex, feeling the warmth of his body. She spooned him, fitting comfortably into the curves of his body. Gigi rubbed her face against the white cotton of his T-shirt, feeling the soft texture, smelling the masculine scent of the man.

Rex stirred.

She slipped her arm around his chest, her hand brushing his curly chest hair as she reached across to the other side. She thought, *I want to keep holding you like this, babe!*

She thought back to the day they became lovers, unlike Gigi's other relationships. Her beauty was her calling card. The men knew it. She knew it. Those relationships usually started based on pure physical attraction, often at first sight. One guy had proposed to her within minutes, unable to contain himself. She had this effect on men. All men.

In her younger days, she had been a wild child, flitting from man to man like a kid in a candy store. She wasn't in the market for a long-term relationship. Men had come and gone, many showering her with expensive gifts, flowers, fancy dinners, money, jewels—you name it. She had fun; what young girl wouldn't?

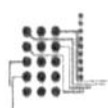

Recently, she had run into someone she once dated. At the time they met, he was already a successful businessman in his mid-thirties.

"Evan?" she asked as he pushed his cart toward her in the store.

He stopped in front of her. "Gigi, how are you?"

"Imagine seeing you." She scrutinized him. Evan appeared a lot older. Still somewhat attractive, but packed with extra pounds and an expanding girth. Perhaps the stress of the job had taken a toll? Maybe he had let himself go, dined on too many rich, calorie-laden meals, slacked off on his exercises? Gotten lazy?

Evan walked around his cart, arms outstretched for a hug. "It's so good to see you!" He seemed genuinely glad.

They had parted on friendly terms. The relationship had fizzled out on its own after the glow faded. Evan moved on, and Gigi did too. But in the time they were together, they sure had fun. They both loved to live it up. He had the money and plenty of it. She made plans, and he went along with it, never squawked about the bill, never stingy, not like some other men.

She pecked him on the cheek before returning his hug. "It's good to see you. How are you?"

"Doing well. I still have the business. Although, I don't travel as much these days. I don't miss it."

"It's been, what, like two or three years?"

He studied her face, a slight frown surfacing on his brow. "You haven't changed a bit." He shifted, peering at the other side of her face, before pronouncing, "Nope, no crow's feet, worry or laugh lines, and not a strand of gray hair."

She laughed. "Don't give me that. It's too early for grays."

"Look at me," he said, pointing at a few streaks at his temples and his waistline. "How do you *not* get this?"

"I must have the right genes," she laughed, shrugging.

"I want some of whatever you're having," he said, half joking, before he straightened up, sucking in his stomach. "You dating anyone now?"

"I am. And it's getting serious."

"Lucky guy," he said, pushing his cart.

As he strolled away down the aisle, Gigi wondered what it'd be like to grow older. How would *she* look?

Chapter 23
DR. KITE

KITE TOILED, FINISHING EARLY IN the morning. He lifted his fingers from the keyboard, after finding the files for the prototype chip, occupying space on his laptop. He rubbed his chin, encountering the slight roughness of his stubble while he thought, rejoicing in this stroke of good luck.

In a small packet tucked away in the zip-locked inner pocket of the laptop bag, he had found the tracker microchip, a basic version he had designed earlier to track medications taken. But in his rush to capitalize on his more glamorous, highly profitable chips, this early model had fallen to the wayside.

"Yes!" he shouted. He pushed his chair back from the desk and dashed to the bathroom, acting on the urgency to pee, his bladder screaming out for relief.

He made his way to the kitchen, washed his hands, and started a pot of coffee. Opening the refrigerator, he rummaged through the items on the almost bare shelves, looking for a quick bite. He found a pack of cheese.

Famished, he snatched it, breaking off the pieces, not bothering to slice it. He gobbled it all up, washing the Monterey Jack down with the freshly brewed coffee.

Wiping his mouth with the back of his hand, he leaned on the counter, scanning his small one-bedroom apartment. A forlorn, solitary coffeepot staked a spot on the kitchen counter. A worn armchair faced a twenty-two-inch TV. A desk in the corner. A narrow hallway bathroom with barely enough room to turn. Out of sight was the bedroom, occupied by a twin-size bed, a small table, a makeshift shelf for his clothes, and a laundry basket on the floor, clothes spilling out.

A beam of light filtered through a single window, bits of airborne dust floating in its path as it reached the distressed wood floor.

Kite closed his eyes. Had it come down to this? Would he be able to claw his way back up?

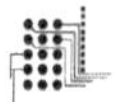

Kite walked across the room and sat at his desk. He caught sight of a pamphlet, partially visible between the papers and tucked inside a larger pocket of the laptop carrier. He flipped through it. Glossy, sexy, like the commercials for drugs treating men who are impotent. First, you see the woman reclined on the bed and your brain links with sex. Enter the man in her life. They have fun together, drinking a glass of wine, sitting in the bathtub, walking together hand in hand, embracing, watching a gorgeous sunset. Fade away.

His fingers probed behind it, in the dark recess of an inner pocket, touching a thumb drive and a foil envelope. He felt the outlines of a capsule as he read the label: "Prototype Number 9." Kite stopped, blood pulsing through his veins.

Trembling and shaking, he carefully opened the sealed packet and peeked inside at the nanobot-coated capsule encasing the new prototype chip. For women and men. Firing up the brain cells and pumping the hormones, orchestrated like a finely tuned piece of machinery, well-oiled and running, all body parts in sync with each other.

But the topping on the cake was its ability to enhance scents—not just any scent, but the most sensual, creating a powerful attraction between a man and woman. A chemical-induced love potion only triggered at the time of implant to capture the unique scents of a man and woman, sending an army of irretrievable nanobots. Multiplied thousandfold. Eros. The ultimate pheromone.

Chapter 24

LILLY

SHE THOUGHT OF THEM AS her recruits. Technically they weren't—yet. Not all would make it. This first round of the program would weed out the unfit, the weakest, the least likely to succeed. For those who made it through, it would be the beginning of the real thing. She nodded, brushing aside a nagging thought. Shouldn't she be telling them now?

She'd learned a lot since the first time. She worked relentlessly to put the program together, making changes after the women showed up, fine-tuning it. She started out with six women in the first class. Four women made it through the two-week program. In the end, she offered the next level. Only two women, Tiffany and Naomi, rose to the challenge and finished the advanced level. Tiffany's assignment? Dr. Kite.

Lilly's thoughts shifted to the newly arrived group of women, the second group. They would be stretched to their limits, physically and mentally. Not just a matter of who was the strongest of them all, but also how tough they were, how cunning, relentless, resilient, adaptable.

She had a few select clients lined up, discreetly. Those clients would never meet the women. It was better this way. She took women who looked like the average population, rather than only the fittest and most athletic. For these jobs, she recruited all kinds of women. But only women.

Lilly put her practical business sense to it. By now she had a firmer grip on it, repeating what worked before, discarding what didn't. These women had given up two weeks of their lives to be here. They knew the scope of the program, but only for the two weeks packed with daily body detox routines, fitness and self-defense training, and sessions to push the limits of physical and mental endurance. After they finished, only a few, the best and brightest, would be offered the chance to move on.

She stopped trying to guess. One thing she'd learned was to expect the unexpected.

"Lilly?" Naomi's voice broke through her thoughts. "We have a little problem."

"Already?" Lilly snapped, irritated at being disturbed. "What is it?"

"It's Hanna." She paused. "A message was left for her."

"What did it say?"

"Her mother said her grandmother had taken a turn for the worse. They're gathering the family together." Naomi added, "She sounded worried, distraught, pressed for time."

"When did she call?"

"A few minutes ago."

"Tell Hanna to come to my office please."

Hanna knocked on the door, entering when Lilly called out.

Seated behind the desk, Lilly gave her a slight nod. Naomi, standing at her side, moved forward to greet Hanna, waving to the empty chair.

"Please sit down."

Hanna hesitated, stepping awkwardly forward. "Am I in trouble?"

"No, not at all. We want to talk to you."

Lilly reached out and pressed a button, replaying the voice mail message from Hanna's mother.

Hanna fidgeted in her chair. "I need to call her back."

"You can," said Lilly. "But you need to decide what you want to do. If you leave the program, you won't be able to come back."

"When do you need my decision?"

"Tomorrow morning, by 10:00 a.m."

Hanna pulled back her chair and stood. "I won't need more time. I've already decided."

Chapter 25

ELLEN

IT HAD BEEN ONE HECK of a day. Ellen looked at the team as they sat around the conference room table and waited for the boss.

Alone in his office, Andrew Capstone tapped his cell phone, ending the call. "Yes!" he shouted. The big Kahuna. He got the contract. Success had eluded him for years. Now he was finally in the big league. His opportunity to swim with the big boys, to get a good exposure on a massive business project, and possibly more work with same guys again in the future.

He leaned back in his chair, fingertips touching. His company, dEsign+, had garnered the coveted project, to interior design and stage the showhomes of Ergon Towers' newest property, the multi-million-dollar condo being built in the swankiest part of town. It would be an expensive project. A lot was riding on showcasing it successfully. Muck it up, and their name would be tarnished.

He pushed back his chair, grabbed his coffee mug, and

walked down the hall to the meeting. His steps were quick and light.

Ellen turned at the sound of the door opening as Andy entered the room.

He set his mug down but remained standing at the head of the table. He surveyed the expectant, upturned faces.

"My father immigrated here at nineteen. All he had in his pockets was some cash his mother stuffed in his hand, money she had saved up. In the old country, he had apprenticed with a master furniture maker at the age of thirteen. When he came here, his dream was to open a furniture store." He paused, recollecting his thoughts. "I remember the first time when he took Mama, my brother, and me to see the place, the building. He wanted to surprise us. He saw beyond the bareness, and it's potential excited him. We had a lot of work to do before the store opened."

He looked around the room, smiling before continuing. "I remember playing there after school. My father called it *his* store—well, technically it was the bank's until he paid it off years later."

Laughter drifted around the room.

Andy put both hands on the edge of the table, leaning forward. "But what impressed me the most was the window display—a white-painted pedestal table set for two, with fine china, glassware, and sterling silverware. Cloth napkins added a classy touch." He looked out the window, thinking back. "My mother came up with this idea. A woman's touch. She even placed fresh-cut flowers on the table. You know what happened?" he asked, raising his eyebrows.

A few heads shook.

"Her display brought in prospective customers. I'll never forget that day, the first day she set it up . . . our store was mobbed."

"Did you work in his store?" someone asked.

"For a while, long enough to know I didn't want the hassle of dealing with inventory. But my older brother, he was made for it." He sighed, standing straight. "I left, went to school, got my degree, and started this company. Now I get to buy furniture and design staging rooms for commercial real estate properties."

"I have something else to share with you," said Andy, throwing a glowing look around the table. "We got the job!" He punctuated his words with emphasis, smiling in triumph, as a round of cheers and applause filled the room.

"Bravo," thundered the man sitting close to Ellen, the sound of his voice piercing her ears.

Ellen caught sight of Andy looking directly at her, flushed with excitement, with the victory. She smiled back, giving him a thumbs-up.

Andy continued to talk, holding his hands up to calm the group. "I want to thank everyone here because *you* did it! Tonight we'll celebrate at O'Brien's Tavern. Tab's on me."

He waited for another round of applause to die down before continuing. "I spoke to an executive at Ergon Towers. They're planning a formal social, an icebreaker, to meet the folks they'll be working with on this project." He waved his hand. "All of you, please mark your calendar for next Saturday night. Any questions?"

"What's the plan going forward?"

"It'll take at least half a dozen meetings to pick cabinets, countertops, fixtures, tiles, toilets, tubs, carpets, color schemes and paint colors. Four model units—a studio, one bedroom, two bedrooms, and three bedrooms—plus an office and reception area. Fully furnished. We'll need to finish first and be in and out of there fast, ahead of sales."

"You all have the packet. Please read it over. We'll meet on Monday morning to outline next steps, flesh out the timeline, iron out some of the issues. Be back here at 9:00 a.m." Andy rose, pausing a moment at Ellen's chair before leaving the room.

Chapter 26
GIGI

THE ROOM WAS DARK, CURTAINS drawn over the window. Still, Gigi could make out the shape of his half-curled body on the bed. "Rex . . .?" she murmured, rubbing his back, not sure if he was awake.

He didn't respond.

She moved closer, slipping one arm around his shoulder, nestling her chin to rest at the hollow between his neck and shoulder. She purred, "Honey, are you awake?"

No sound, no movement.

She blew in his ear, knowing how much he liked it, trying to coax him awake. "Rrrrex."

This time, a slight stir, then a shake of the head.

"Rex," she repeated, louder, her hand shaking his shoulder.

"Leave me alone," mumbled Rex, quickly burying his face back in the pillow as he shook his shoulder to shrug off her hand.

"What's wrong?"

Pulling the bed covers up over his ears, Rex leaned away from her.

"Oh, for Pete's sake!" said Gigi. "I don't know what's wrong with you." She bent to grab her clothes strewn on the floor.

Fighting the temptation to go back, she stomped out of the room, making sure to have the last word. "Seriously, Rex, you suck!"

Chapter 27

ELLEN

"MAY I JOIN YOU?" SAID Andy, a drink in one hand.

Ellen looked up, dabbed the napkin on her lips before answering. "Of course, have a seat." She had snagged a small table at the back of the tavern, having joined the party late.

She had been on the phone talking to her mom, making arrangements for her to stay to take care of Angie again. Ellen had promised to give her a heads-up, but this request came in the afternoon, and her mom was not too pleased with the late notice. Ellen had pleaded with her, telling her about the special occasion, an after-work happy hour to celebrate.

When she finally made her way inside the tavern, the party was already in full swing. The dark room of the wood-paneled bar capably held the noise level of a lively, boisterous crowd. She took a few minutes to adjust and locate the rest of the group seated in the crowded, large booths.

Ellen had stopped to greet a few people, making congratulatory remarks as she made her way through the busy tavern, searching for a small table.

Her food had just arrived when Andy stopped by.

"I'm glad you came."

"Yes, well I can only stay for a short while," said Ellen, toying with her napkin. "But I wanted to be here."

He smiled. "We couldn't have done it without your help."

She perked up, taking a celery stalk and dipping it in rich, thick blue cheese dressing, swirling it before taking a bite.

"I liked your story," said Ellen.

"It's true. My father, you would've liked him."

"He passed?"

"A few years ago. My mother is still alive," said Andy.

"And you have a brother?"

"He still runs Dad's company and works there. He never married."

She crunched on the celery.

He watched her lips move.

"Have some," she said, pushing the plate toward him. "This is the juiciest, crisp celery, and the dip is delicious."

"Already had some with my wings."

"I just have celery."

"You didn't order wings?

"I've changed my diet, cutting out meat. Lots of vegetables, fruits, and nuts."

"Recently?"

"When I found out I was pregnant." She paused. "I made other changes in my life."

He nodded, encouraging her.

"So pregnancy was my inspiration. I was determined to form good habits, to do it right." She paused between another bite of the celery stalk and smiled. "And I feel much better, and healthier."

"Your husband . . ."

"Oh, I'm not married."

"I was going to say he's a lucky man."

She smiled again, looking intently at an imaginary spot on the table.

"I know one thing."

"Oh?" She raised her head.

"You're the best executive assistant I've ever had."

Ellen blushed.

"You don't have to say anything. I want you to know how much I appreciate you." He raised his drink. "Let's have a toast, shall we?"

"I'm not drinking alcohol."

"What are you having?"

"Iced tea." She raised her glass to meet his as his eyes sought hers.

The clink made a pleasant chime. "To us," Andy said, quickly adding, "and to health, happiness, and success."

Chapter 28

DR. KITE

HE GLANCED AT HIS CELL phone, willing it to ring, for her to call. He held back from calling her, even though they had exchanged phone numbers after she got home from the doctor's office. He replayed the last exchange they had over and over in his mind—how she looked, what she said, the way she looked at him. He knew something had been communicated between them, a slight spark. He was sure of it.

She didn't protest when he offered to check up on her. But he wouldn't show up at her apartment unannounced. He'd call first. He didn't want to mess anything up, to upset her. She needed to rest last night, so he didn't disturb her.

Once again, he checked the time on his phone. Tiffany had told him today's her day off, and it worked out perfectly after her dizzy spill yesterday for her to stay at home.

Maybe he should take her something to eat? He got up to pace the small room. No longer content to stay there. Itching to take action, to do something for her, for his Tiffany.

Kite picked up his phone. He had already entered her name, number, and address in his contacts. He added her name to his favorites list too. The only name on the list. He called her. Will she pick up on the first ring? Before it goes into voice mail? He pressed the phone against his ear, willing her to answer. It seemed like an eternity, the wait, but in reality, only seconds ticking by.

"Hello."

"Oh," he gushed. "I'm so glad you're there. How are you feeling?"

"Kite? Is that you?" Her voice came across faint, weak.

"Yes, remember yesterday? I said I'd call."

"Ah," she murmured.

"I thought I'd come by, you know, to bring you some food."

"Now's not a good time."

"I'm sorry. I didn't mean to—I thought I'd check in on you."

A pause at the other end, followed by a sigh. "Maybe later."

"Later is good. What time?"

"Hmm, let's see, mid-afternoon perhaps."

"Three o'clock?" He held his ear closer to the phone, hearing something muffled in the background. "Are you there?"

"Yeah, okay," she said before she disconnected.

Five hours. Kite would see Tiffany today.

He rubbed his hands in glee, overcome with excitement. He had time to take a shower, make a list, go shopping and pick up a few items.

He recalled their conversation yesterday when they went to the pharmacy to pick up her medication. She didn't want him to go at first. He insisted on going and paying for it. She relented in the end. She should know better now to take it on time, on schedule, every day. He'd make sure to stress this again when he saw her this afternoon. He straightened up, the doctor in him taking over, switching to thinking of her as his patient now.

He decided to tell her about himself, to reveal what he'd been hiding from her. He had an ulterior motive. He patted his pocket, feeling the outlines of the two injection pens, one holding the tracker medication chip inside and the other the Number 9 microchip.

Would she let him implant the chips? He'd explain. Tell her it'd be for her own good. She'd have total control over how long she wanted it. He would remove it at any time if she told him.

It seemed like forever since he'd seen Tiffany, but only yesterday. Kite checked the time on his cell phone more often than was healthy.

After toweling his hair, he stepped out of the shower and dried his trim body. Although middle age had crept up on him, he'd been careful not to put on too much weight. He wiped the mirror, clearing the fog with his forearm, and studied his face, glimpsing the strong jaw now rid of his beard. He rubbed the five o'clock shadow. Time to get out his shaving cream.

Chapter 29

ELLEN

THE WEEK FLEW BY. ELLEN was buried in the flurry of activity, working with the team to get the staging design project started. By the week's end, they had worked out a reasonable schedule, outlined tasks, added milestones and deliverable dates.

Andy provided input and guidance when needed as he reviewed the drafts they prepared before approving the document. When Friday rolled around, they met in the conference room again.

"You guys delivered," Andy said as he started off the meeting. He loosened his tie and relaxed, sitting back in the chair. "I know you're looking forward to the social tomorrow, so I'll make this short."

A few nods went around the table.

"I've sent the report. A meeting is being scheduled next week with all parties involved from both companies." He paused. "I got a call, right before this meeting. Unofficial feedback."

Ellen leaned forward. She hadn't heard this part.

"They liked the report. Tomorrow night, at the social, they will announce the managers and introduce the people you'll be working with."

Excited murmurs rippled around the table, and a few shouts.

But Andy wasn't done yet. "I have something for you." He opened his briefcase, retrieved a stack of envelopes labeled with names, and passed them out.

"What's this?" several people asked.

"Go ahead, open it."

Ellen pulled apart the flap, opening the envelope. Around her, the sounds of tearing paper filled the air. She peeked inside, seeing a check. A closer look revealed the number. She gulped, holding the envelope against her chest. A quick look around the table affirmed similar reactions, as a chorus of "Thank yous" sounded, joined by laughter.

Not bad. The little black dress screamed classy, sexy. Ellen swirled, tossing her shoulder-length hair back. Tonight she'd leave her hair down, the thick brown waves cascading in luxurious layers. She turned, glancing at her side views, feeling the soft tickle of her hair brushing the nape of her neck and shoulder. Feminine. All feminine.

She slipped on her earrings, the long, sparkly ones dangling four inches from her ears. Putting on the finishing touch—a bold pink lipstick—she clicked the case shut. Her manicured fingers dropped the tube in her purse. Ellen took a breath, straightened her dress, and headed to the living room to say goodbye to her mom and baby Angie.

"Wow, Ellen." Mrs. Fulbright's look was admiring, approving.

"Mom, it's my new dress. I'm down to a size six now." Ellen beamed as she preened to show off her figure.

"Your other clothes?"

"I took them down to that place the church opened for women getting back on their feet, getting back to work, The Restocked Closet."

"Sounds like you won't ever need them again."

Ellen shook her head as she reached for the baby in her mom's arms. "Angie!"

The baby gurgled and laughed in her arms.

Ellen hugged her baby and rubbed noses with her. Angie still had a bit of pudginess on her face. Ellen inhaled, catching a faint whiff of the baby's scent, remembering how she loved Angie's new baby smell. Holding Angie's tiny fingers in the palm of her hand, Ellen kissed them. She held Angie close, feeling the warmth of her little body as she lovingly caressed the fine, baby curls on her head.

Angie giggled, her dimpled hand reaching out to pat Ellen's face.

Ellen's mom gave a discreet cough, interrupting as she pointed to the clock.

"I know," said Ellen, reluctant to give up this moment.

"This is your big night."

"Our big night."

"Are you excited?"

"I just want to relax and have fun."

"And Andy?"

"Andy's my boss," Ellen said defensively.

"You've been mentioning his name quite often lately."

"He's *my boss*."

"That's all he is?"

"I have to go," said Ellen with a departing smile. She gave Angie one more hug before leaving.

Chapter 30

ELLEN

ERGON TOWERS HOSTED THE SOCIAL event at the Angora Hotel. One glance told Ellen they spared no expense. The decorations, the singer and the musicians on the stage, the flutes of champagne, the delicate, fancy *hors d'oeuvres* atop of silver plates making their way around the room.

Everyone was dressed up, out to make a good first impression. Even the man with the paunch popping his shirt buttons wore a new suit, a size bigger to contain his sizable girth.

She touched her dress, feeling the expensive, soft material hugging her hips. Well worth every penny.

"Ma'am, would you like one?"

She turned to the waiter and glanced at the champagne glasses. "I believe I will." Ellen reached for a flute.

"Hi," said Andy, appearing suddenly at her side.

Ellen caught her breath. *Who is this gorgeous man?* Indeed not the Andy she knew, her boss, sporting a flattering haircut, dressed impeccably in a slim dark suit, crisp white shirt, and a stunning silk tie.

"You're here," said Andy. He feigned innocence; hiding the fact he'd arrived early, thirty minutes ago, eyes on the entrance, watching for her appearance.

"I'm a few minutes late."

She caught a whiff of his faint masculine scent as she moved closer for the hug. She was unprepared at the pleasing splash he stirred on her senses—the sight, sound, touch, and smell.

"You look amazing," said Andy. He nodded to the waiter before picking up a champagne glass for himself.

"You aren't looking so bad yourself," said Ellen. She touched his lapel in a teasing way. Her fingers traced it to the edge, feeling the smooth fabric. "Good taste." She reinforced her approval with a smile.

"Hey, Ellen," called Jeremy, one of the guys on her team. He was standing with a group of four, gathered in a circle. Three men, one woman. She recognized two of them from her group.

"Come and meet some new folks from Ergon Towers."

She moved away from Andy, walking toward them. Her confidence radiated. She was on top of her game. Their admiring glances bolstered her, and the selection of her dress played no small part.

The circle parted to welcome her. They made small talk, getting to know one another. "I'm Harry," one of them said, peering at her through black-framed glasses.

"Hi, I'm Ellen. Pleased to meet you."

"Enjoying this?" said Harry, waving his hand across the room.

"Nice party here."

"The company likes to do this in grand style."

"You've been with them long?"

"Oh, about eight months," said Harry.

"So you're new."

"Ergon Towers has been expanding and hiring new people."

"Business is good?"

"It's fantastic!"

"What department are you in?" said Ellen.

"Real estate. Condo development and sales."

"Your background?"

"In construction. And yours?"

"I have some interior decorating experience, but my title now is Executive Assistant to the Director," said Ellen.

"You like that kind of work?"

"It's frustrating at times, I'll admit. But you have to be patient and be willing to work with people, see their perspectives, and find solutions."

"Sounds like you have your work cut out for you," said Harry.

"I enjoy working with people," said Ellen, laughing.

"The challenges are there, for sure. But the payoff, when it comes, is tremendous. Our multi-million dollar projects provide jobs not only for the construction industry but many others in the community."

Ellen nodded while enjoying a bite of the smoked salmon with herbed crème fraîche on her plate. "I take it our company is only one among others you'll be working with?"

"Your company is one of the most important. The design showroom is what the public sees. Design it right, and you'll have interested buyers. You offer the vision of a home they admire, want, *have* to have."

"We create curb appeal for the showroom," said Ellen. She paused. "So you'll be our contact on this project?"

"I'll be one of the contacts, as the assistant. My boss is the project manager."

"Is he here tonight?"

He craned his neck to scan the room. Being tall and gangly, he had a better view. "There he is," said Harry. He waved, catching someone's attention, gesturing to him to come over.

Ellen couldn't make him out yet.

Harry nudged her to make room in their circle for the newcomer. Turning to Ellen, he said, "Brad, my boss."

Reaching out to shake his hand, Ellen froze in midair. *Brad? Is it him? Her Brad? The father of her baby?* She hadn't seen Brad since their night together. She hadn't told him about their baby.

Chapter 31

LILLY

SHE TOOK HER RED PEN and crossed out Hanna's name.

Pushing the folder aside, she called Tiffany.

"Hello?"

"It's Lilly."

"We're making progress," said Tiffany. "He's coming over this afternoon."

"Your medicine, you stopped taking it?"

"Until I got dizzy the other day and the doctor figured it out."

"You feeling better?"

"I'm back on the meds, courtesy of Kite."

"He doesn't suspect?"

"He doesn't have a clue."

"He may be down and out, but remember, he's no dummy."

"Ha! He may be a genius," said Tiffany, laughing. "But he hasn't figured this out. Right now his heart is telling him what he wants."

"The old fool."

"He's not that old. When he's cleaned up, he looks much better."

"But he looked like a bum when you first met him at the grocery store?"

"He *was* a bum, down and out."

"You holding out okay?"

"Yeah, I thought I wouldn't like it here, moving to a small town, leaving the big city."

"And?"

"It slowly grew on me. When I have a day off, I walk along the beach. It's better than medication."

"I'm sorry about your mother."

"I miss her terribly," said Tiffany. She pinched her lips before she bitterly spat out, "She didn't have to die."

Lilly gave her a moment of silence before she spoke again. "I'm very sorry."

"I need time. You know what they say, time heals all wounds."

"Tiffany, I meant to say this, you're like a daughter to me. The daughter I never had." Lilly hesitated. "I don't mean any disrespect. But I'd like to think we're family now."

"I want you to leave me alone too."

"I have since you left the city," said Lilly, thinking about the times she'd picked up her phone and thought of calling her. "I've missed—"

"Enough of this," snapped Tiffany.

"Look, it's a big step forward, what he's doing today, coming to your apartment," said Lilly soothingly.

"No crap. I didn't want Kite to come. But this will move things along much faster."

"Are you sure he doesn't suspect?"

"He thinks I'm a babe waiting for my knight in shining armor," said Tiffany with a hoot. Her laughter faded as she added, "He sounded so disappointed when I first turned him down this morning."

For a moment, Lilly's thoughts flashed back to the night at Duggers, the restaurant where she first met Kite. He was a man of charm, all polished exterior, revealing a glint of the boyish softness inside he tried so well to hide. The man who said to her, 'Tonight is this lady's lucky night,' and '*my* lucky day.' They were both down on their luck that night. She had nothing more to give to him except for a seat at her table.

He paid her attention, listened to each word she uttered, made her laugh, made her forget her pain, gave her hope, made her *want* to live again, to fight her way back to life instead of giving up on it, on herself. She clung to the hope, fixated on it, desperate for the prototype mind-control chip, his magic bullet for all her troubles. She finally called Kite, and he implanted the chip.

She believed Kite when he offered her a way out, an end to the bitterness left behind by her divorce, by another man who took her for all he could, then discarded her, casting her away in one fell swoop without another glance. The infidelity, the betrayal, the baby he had with the other woman, all were egregious. But it was the cruelty wrought by someone she loved, trusted, and devoted her life to that hurt the most, and being reduced to nothing, not even an afterthought. She shook her head to banish her past.

"Be careful," Lilly told Tiffany. "He may seem like a fool,

an old fool. But don't ever let down your guard."

Tiffany snorted and coughed as she tried to catch her breath. "You haven't seen him like this. Men! Such fools!"

"He might try to inject you with his chips."

"What? I thought you said everything burned up in the warehouse fire?"

"You never know. What if Kite's got some stashed elsewhere, like hidden?"

"I'll be careful. I mean, Kite's already paid for my medication, and I'm supposed to be getting better. There's nothing he can do. So if all he wants is to see me for a few minutes this afternoon, I'll play along with it."

"I don't trust men," said Lilly.

Chapter 32

GIGI

THEY SAY PRETTY GIRLS HAVE trouble showing love, giving love. She'd known beautiful girls like that. She was one of them.

Gigi poured steaming coffee into the mug. Her fingers curled around the ceramic handle while with her other hand she rubbed the smooth glaze. She sipped, testing the temperature.

She replayed the scene with Rex. In all the time she'd known him, he'd never acted this way—turned his back on her in bed. Correction. In the *short time* since they'd started sleeping together. Okay, they'd been friends for a long time. They'd only been intimate for a little more than three months. She frowned. *Aren't they still in the bloom, in the rosy period?*

Everything had been great up to this point. Rex had surprised her with this trip. *He's so sweet and romantic,* she thought. She took a long sip of coffee and peeked down the hallway to the bedroom. No sight of him yet.

On the airplane, he had the window seat. Rex had flipped the armrest up and scooted her closer, lifting her legs over his lap, hugging her all during the flight. The stewardess had left them alone.

She had been so excited about seeing this little piece of heaven in the mountains. God's country, wildlife roaming the land. Transported to this place—the city became a distant memory. She could stay here in this idyllic, beautiful land.

Back to Rex. If only she could recapture the magic of the first three months; it had been better than any relationship she ever had. Even though her body went through the motions—the hugs, kisses, the whispered sweet nothings on the pillow, the sex—she had held back. She didn't fake it. She did it willingly. But she wasn't *all* in.

In her past relationships, the men were so grateful for her, the most beautiful and perfect girl they could have, and they were willing to settle for half a heart or less. Her relationships never lasted for long, and when they ended, she did feel sad. Sad not because of a broken heart although sometimes it felt that way, but sorry for the ending. For every beginning, there was an ending in the circle of life. Rex was there to comfort her, to get her through, to make it all better. She never had to wait long, never had a shortage of men.

Rex, he was different. She knew it. As her lover, he wanted her, all of her. Body, heart, and soul. Gigi sighed, feeling the warmth of the mug, wanting more, wanting his warmth again. Could she give him her all?

Chapter 33

ELLEN

HER HANDS SHOOK, AND SHE tipped her plate, sliding the appetizer right off onto her dress. Turning to Brad, she mumbled a "Hi, pleased to meet you" greeting before dashing off to the ladies' room to get a towel and wipe her dress. No one was at the sink. Ellen put out her hands, leaning against the counter, steadying herself for a moment. *Did he recognize her?* It was the last place she'd expected to run into Brad. She hadn't thought of him for a long time.

He looked great, even better than she remembered. Her stomach fluttered. A flicker of memory popped up, uninvited. Brad naked. The taste of his mouth. The feel of his tongue on her lips, pressing and insistent. Their legs intertwined. She suppressed it, fought it.

The flushing of a toilet interrupted her thoughts. She moved toward the last stall, the large handicapped one with a sink. Grabbing a paper towel, she wet it and wiped her dress, careful not to make it worse. Alone where she wouldn't have to face Brad, she steadied her nerves. She splashed some water on her face, thinking back to the conversation with her mother when she'd asked, "Does Brad know?" *No, she never told him about the baby.* After the night when they had sex, she had wrapped the sheet around her and ran out of the bedroom. She stayed locked up in the bathroom for a long time, not coming out until she was sure he had left.

He had called her. But she didn't answer. He had texted her. She didn't respond. He came to her home and knocked. She didn't open the door. Eventually, he'd stopped.

She spun around, surveying her dress in the mirror. The small damp spot where she'd wiped was barely noticeable. She pulled her shoulders up, turned around, and marched out of the bathroom.

"Ellen!" Brad called out from where he was casually standing a few feet away from the bathroom door.

"You remember me," said Ellen cautiously as she walked toward him.

"I wasn't sure at first, but the guys told me your name," said Brad. He stepped closer to her. "You're looking great." He smiled and looked around. "Is there a quiet place we can talk for a few minutes?"

"I noticed some empty meeting rooms. We can go to one of them." Ellen led the way. Down the hallway, they found a small room with a few rows of chairs and a podium, which was vacant at the moment.

"This'll do," said Brad as he plopped down in a front-row chair and gestured to Ellen.

"Brad."

"You left me hanging." He got right to the point.

"Long story."

"What the hell happened? I opened my eyes, and you were gone."

"I . . ."

"Don't you remember?"

"Which part?" Ellen couldn't resist a tease, even as her voice cracked. "The restaurant?"

"You damn well know what I meant!"

"I'm sorry I didn't return your calls."

"The night we had sex," Brad said and paused. "You remember, don't you?" He persisted. "My eyes were still closed, but all of a sudden your body changed . . . You became heavier, and larger like you gained weight. When I opened my eyes, you were gone. Locked yourself in the bathroom."

Ellen was silent. The moment she'd dreaded had come. She struggled to get the words out, but couldn't. Her hand gripped the arm of the chair; the skin stretched tightly over her knuckles.

He walked to a table with a pitcher of ice water and a row of stacked glasses. As he poured, the cubes tumbled into the glass. "Drink this," he said.

"Thanks," said Ellen, shooting him a grateful look. She took a long gulp, the ice hitting her teeth, the cold water rushing past, traveling down her throat.

"Feel better?"

She nodded. "I owe you an apology." She mustered a weak smile. "It felt crazy scary. I locked myself in the bathroom. I looked in the mirror. Realized I was back to my size."

Brad frowned, shaking his head. "I'm confused. So you gained back your weight?"

"Every pound of it and more," said Ellen.

"I don't understand. How could it have happened so quickly?"

"You see, I got an implant, a microchip, and lost weight. I was given a deadline to make good on the offer before the time expired." She spread her hands, palms up in a pleading gesture. "I missed my deadline, 8:30 p.m. that night, while we were having sex. I didn't pay, so the chip expired, and my weight reverted."

"Wait, you got implanted with a microchip? What did it do?"

"It adjusted my metabolism to what I ate. It worked on a cellular level, regulating the mitochondria."

"So it worked, right? When I met you, you were slim."

"Yes, but?"

"But why did you gain your weight back all of a sudden?"

"I knew in the back of my mind it was too good to be true."

"So you had no idea?" Brad persisted, trying to understand.

"Well, yes and no." Ellen paused. "I was given a one-time offer of a free trial period."

"And then what happened?"

"It had an expiration date and time." Ellen licked her lips, which suddenly seemed dry. She took a drink of the ice water before she continued. "I had to pay before it expired."

It finally dawned on Brad. "Let me guess . . . It expired when we were having sex."

Ellen nodded, whispering, "Yes."

"You figured it out then?"

"No, later, after I had cried my heart out and calmed down." She shot Brad an imploring look. "But I couldn't face you, so I took the easy way out."

"I worried about you, but you cut me off." He snapped.

"I'm sorry."

"I thought I'd done something to make you mad."

"I couldn't face you—you would have freaked out if you saw me," said Ellen, brushing a wisp of hair off her forehead. She had practiced multiple scenes, each a bit different, of how she'd tell him, what she'd say if they ever met. She knew she had waited too long.

"Why didn't you call me later?" Brad insisted. "It's been over a year. Did you think to pick up the phone at any time to call me? You had my number. You could have texted me, left me a message. Anything." Agitated, he stood up, pacing back and forth.

"Brad." Her well-planned speeches melted by the wayside. Her excuses seemed pathetic. She thought, *Should I come clean now? When I'm face to face with him?*

Something in her voice, her tone, her look, grabbed him. Brad stopped pacing.

"Please. Please, sit down. I'm not finished yet," said

Ellen. She made her decision.

Brad stared at her, thinking, *What else hasn't she told me?*

"There is something else you need to know."

He was curious. "Tell me everything now." He waited. A muscle twitched in his cheek as he clenched his teeth.

"Brad, you're a father."

"*What?*" He spat out the word, stunned.

"The time we were together, the *one time* . . . I became pregnant."

"A baby—" Brad's mouth dropped open.

"*Our* baby, Brad."

"Boy or girl?" he whispered.

"A girl, Angie."

"You named her Angie." He choked up.

"Yes," Ellen whispered.

"I'm a . . . father" stammered Brad, stopping to soak it all in. He sank into the seat. His head was spinning, flooded with a mixture of emotions—anger, confusion, shock.

Ellen recalled the moment she found out she was pregnant, alone in her bathroom with the test strips. *A single mom*, she'd thought. She had wept. Scared to face the future, wondering if she was cut out to be a mom. She didn't ask for it, hadn't expected it. She'd crawled back into bed, under the comfort and safety of the covers.

She stayed in bed all day. She slept, cried, and slept again. Ellen stared at the ceiling when she woke and cried again. She placed her hand over her belly, moving across the flatness until it stilled, resting over the life she carried inside.

Chapter 34

DR. KITE

THREE O'CLOCK. KITE STOOD IN front of Tiffany's door. He pushed his shoulders back, balancing the bags he carried to reach out and ring the bell.

"Coming," said a faint voice from inside.

He waited, fixing a smile on his face.

The door flung open.

He moved forward, eager to thrust the bouquet of fragrant roses toward her. His smile was beaming.

"What's this?" said Tiffany, surprised.

"Get well flowers," said Kite.

"Come on in while I get them in water."

Kite relaxed. Carrying the bags, he followed her into the kitchen and set them on the counter. "I bought some groceries and take-out food," said Kite, quickly adding, "for when you feel like eating."

Tiffany filled a vase, plunked in the long-stemmed flowers, and stooped to smell the roses. "These are lovely."

Kite beamed.

"Let me put the groceries away, and then I'll make a pot of coffee. Would you like a cup?"

"Oh yes, and there's some vanilla biscotti to go with it," said Kite, gesturing toward the groceries.

Tiffany grabbed a plate from the cabinet and pushed it toward him. "Here, you put those on the plate while I finish what I'm doing."

Kite couldn't help thinking, *This is a sliver of domestic heaven. Dare I hope?* He snuck a few glances at her while she wasn't looking. She was the picture of casual chic, the kind he saw in magazines while flipping the pages at the checkout line. Seemingly without effort, she managed to be elegant yet comfy casual, exuding warmness yet keeping her distance. Her beauty was quite remarkable.

He suddenly became awkward, his palms sweaty.

"Hey, you okay?" Her voice close to his ear startled him.

He nodded.

"Thought your mind had gone with that blank look," said Tiffany, propelling him toward the living room sofa. "You sure you don't want something else?"

"I'm okay with the biscotti and coffee."

She hovered over him, fussed a bit to make sure he was comfortable.

He patted his coat pocket, making sure the injection pens were in place. He'd brought both of the chips, the one for the medication reminders, and the other one—for love.

Chapter 35
GIGI

SHE TOOK ANOTHER SPOONFUL OF the sinfully rich ice cream loaded with chocolate bits, nuts, and caramel swirls. Gigi had grabbed the container and flipped open the lid, eating straight from the cardboard carton. Her go-to comfort food, any time of the day.

She barely looked up when Rex appeared, dressed in a white T-shirt and blue jeans. She quickly shoved more ice cream into her mouth.

"Leaving some for me?" said Rex.

She tipped it toward him, showing the almost empty carton, then scooped up the last bit of ice cream. Licking her lips, she smacked them for emphasis as she finished. She plunked the spoon in the carton and walked to the sink, tossing them both in.

Rex had an urge to shake her, to punish her for her childish act. The clink of the metal as the spoon spilled into the sink sounded loud in the quiet kitchen. But he couldn't deny his part in it. Brushing her off in bed this morning earned him this. Man up.

"Is this our first fight?"

"You could say that."

"We need to talk," said Rex. He dragged another chair beside her.

She got up to fill her coffee mug, taking her time with it before sitting down again.

Rex shifted in his seat. "I'm sorry about this morning."

Her icy gaze was unforgiving.

He twisted to face her. "I haven't been honest with you."

Gigi jabbed her finger in his chest, making sure he could feel her nail. "You turned your back on me."

"I was doubled over in pain."

She stopped pressing her nail and drew back her hand in midair, cocking her head to one side. "You . . . you're sick?"

He nodded, his gaze holding hers. "I didn't want to spoil this trip. I thought I could hide it—until afterward."

"So this morning?" She let out a long breath out, grappling with this.

"Yeah. I had overexerted myself. My body reacted. I was in pain."

"How . . . how long has it been?" Gigi whispered.

"It's recent."

"What's wrong?"

He shrugged. "I went to see a doctor before we left. He drew my blood and ordered some tests."

"So you don't know the results yet?"

"I'll find out soon. I've got an appointment after we get back."

"I'm so sorry," said Gigi as her eyes moistened. She thought, *How can I have acted so shamefully, so selfishly?*

Epilogue

Chapter 36
GIGI

GIGI MOVED CLOSER TO STAND in front of Rex, still in his chair at the kitchen counter. Her thighs pressed into his knees as she leaned in, gazing into his eyes. Silently she pleaded forgiveness and at the same time expressed affection and concern.

He wiped the dampness at the corner of her eye with his thumb. As he gazed at her face, his heart beat faster, pumping fresh oxygen into his bloodstream, bringing renewed energy, dulling the pain for a moment. His knees parted, arms raised to wrap her in his embrace.

"I love you, Gigi," said Rex. His voice cracked. He buried his head in her long hair.

"I love you too," said Gigi. She hadn't been put to the test yet, but having said it felt reassuring and gave it teeth. Would she have the strength to support him?

Her thoughts churned back to the times when he was her rock—when she was ill, the car accident, her nightmares.

Gigi stiffened, pulling back to look at Rex, as her thoughts twirled back to the past. The day Rex picked her up at the Hotel Seven, frantic, after searching for her all night when she didn't come home. Her memory was fuzzy after the car accident. Rex had called his friend, Steve Cosine, for help. Steve was a consultant and sometimes a private investigator who retired from the force. He'd found her car abandoned near the Highway 15 underpass after the accident.

"Rex?" snapped Gigi as these thoughts triggered her memory. Back to earlier, when she glimpsed the email—why she'd rushed outside to tell him.

She made an abrupt turn, hurrying back to the bedroom to retrieve the laptop. Carrying it to the kitchen, she set it on the counter and opened it. A few days ago, Rex had insisted on exchanging email passwords in case something happened. She had thought it odd at the time, but it made sense now—his illness.

She clicked on the mail icon and waited for it to load up. "I came outside that morning to tell you something."

"When I was chopping wood," said Rex, nodding. "What was it?"

"An email. The subject line caught my attention."

"Did you read it?"

"No, I ran to get you," said Gigi, shaking her head. "Something about my accident. In your inbox."

She peered, staring intently at the screen as she scrolled through the messages until she found it.

She stopped, pushing the laptop toward Rex.

She pointed to the still unopened email.

He paused.

"Go ahead," Gigi urged him.

Rex clicked open the email from his buddy Steve, the private investigator. He read the one sentence out loud.

Gigi grabbed his hands, stifling a wave of fear as an episode of her life, one she tried to forget, came back to haunt her.

From: Steve Cosine

To: Rex Masden

Subject: GIGI'S Accident - Important Information

We have a match on fingerprints taken from the van used to transport Gigi to Hotel Seven.

Steve

Chapter 37

ELLEN

IT WAS TEN O'CLOCK WHEN she made it home. She had texted her mom.

Ellen kicked off her shoes as she stepped in the doorway. Her mom was still up, watching TV, laughing at an old *I Love Lucy* re-run.

"Hi, Mom."

"How did it go?"

"I'll tell you in a minute. I want to check on Angie first."

She opened the door to Angie's room. The baby was sleeping, snug in her bed. Ellen walked in, her bare feet not making a sound. She smiled, staying there a few minutes, watching Angie sleep, listening to her gentle snores.

When Ellen returned to the living room, her mom had turned off the TV and was waiting for her.

"I can tell something happened tonight," said her mom. She patted the couch. "Come, sit down and talk to me."

No longer a child, Ellen asserted herself as a thirty-six-year-old woman. "I don't want to hear any criticisms from you. I've had enough tonight," said Ellen as she sat next to her mom on the couch. Close, but not touching. "I saw Brad tonight."

"Brad? You mean Angie's father?"

Ellen nodded. "Surprise of my life. At the social, I met people from the company who hired us for their real estate properties. One of the guys introduced me to his manager, who I'll be working with."

"And it's Brad?"

"Yup. I froze. I spilled food on my dress and ran into the ladies room to clean up. He was outside, waiting when I walked out."

"No escaping this time."

"He made sure of it," said Ellen. "So we talked. He was angry at first. He had a right to be. I behaved badly. So I told him about the microchip, why I didn't, *couldn't* face him." She paused. "He had a lot to soak in, but I told him more."

"About Angie?"

"Yes, about our baby."

"Was it the right decision?"

"I went with my gut feeling at the moment. Brad's the baby's father."

"Wait, did you lie to me?" She paused. "You told me Brad was out of the picture. You led me to believe he knew about Angie but chose not to be part of Angie's life."

"I didn't say that."

"Which is it?" she scoffed. "I want the truth, not any pathetic lies."

"Mom, I didn't lie," cried Ellen.

"You're angry. Please calm down."

"No, *you* listen to me. I don't want you to interrupt," said Ellen. "How would you know how I feel? Huh?" She stuck her chin out. "And how scared I was when I found out I was pregnant. I was clueless. I doubted myself, wondered if I could do it."

Ellen patted her stomach. "It seemed unreal in the beginning. My stomach showed no signs for weeks. But one day I felt life, knew for sure my baby was alive." She closed her eyes to recapture the moment. "I knew, when I felt my baby kick me. It became the turning point, changed my life. I became focused on becoming a mother, the best I could be, for my baby. I started loving the pregnancy. The idea of being a single mom took root firmly. I became proud of it. Protective of my baby. I relished the rest of my pregnancy. I laughed. I cried hopeful, happy tears."

"But you—"

"I made excuses. I didn't have the guts to pick up the phone and call him," said Ellen. She crossed her arms and straightened up on the couch. "I had the chance to tell him face to face tonight. I made the decision."

"How did Brad take it?"

"He was overwhelmed. Caught off guard. Didn't see it coming."

"How did you feel?"

"Nervous, but honestly, I'm glad I did. I couldn't have picked a better moment to tell Brad. What perfect timing."

"So what did you guys—"

"We are taking baby steps, Mom."

"And the next step?"

"He wants to meet Angie. I've invited him here."

"When?"

"Tomorrow. Brad's going to get back to me about the time."

"You think he'll follow through after he's had some time to think about it?"

"It's up to him. I gave him my phone number and address again, in case he doesn't have it anymore."

"You've done all you can."

"Now it's up to Brad."

Chapter 38

LILLY

The call from Tiffany never came. Lilly kept the cell phone on her all afternoon just in case. By early evening, she still hadn't heard from her. She called Naomi.

"Naomi, I need your help," said Lilly. "Something is wrong."

"Did you talk to Tiffany?"

"Couldn't get hold of her."

A pause at the other end. "I'm worried," said Naomi.

"She was supposed to meet him at three."

"What happened when you tried calling her?"

"It went straight to voicemail."

"I'm going to drive over there. Should arrive by ten, ten thirty at the latest."

"Be careful," said Lilly. *Something must have happened to Tiffany. Why hasn't she called?*

Chapter 39

DR. KITE

HE LOVED DIPPING BISCOTTI IN his steaming mug full of coffee, and dip he did, not realizing how hungry he was. Kite had been excited about seeing Tiffany again and forgot to eat. Laughing to hide the rumble in his stomach, he snatched another one.

Tiffany finished hers and sat back to watch Kite. She plopped both feet on the edge of the coffee table, feeling the stretch.

"When was the last time you ate a proper meal?"

"Oh, if you counted a microwave dinner last night?"

"No," said Tiffany, planting her feet on the floor now, giving a stomp. "I mean a home-cooked meal."

He shook his head. "I, um . . ."

"If you had to think so hard—."

"Do you remember the first time we met?"

Tiffany's eyes widened. She remembered the day when he first came to the store. She had learned how to make chili when they gave her a card with the recipe printed on it. The first batch she'd messed up. She had to pitch it and start over.

"Because I remember every detail," said Kite.

Tiffany suppressed a response. She had caught sight of him hanging beyond the circle of people crowding around her kiosk. His scruffy appearance, the rumpled clothes. How could she not remember? Was he looking for the closest thing he had to a home-cooked meal that day?

Kite was sitting on her couch now, smiling at her, his cheeks clean-shaven, teeth freshly brushed with peppermint toothpaste. His face, childlike in its eagerness, upturned toward her. The change was more than physical. Something deep inside, the child in him, had surfaced.

"When I was in college, I had a part-time job as a nurse's aide at the rehab center," said Kite. "We took care of men and women. The patients, grateful to have help, didn't complain. The staff, we helped each other out." Kite dabbed his mouth with a napkin, wiping away some imaginary crumbs.

"You liked the work?"

"I didn't hate it. The older patients were nice to me. A few of them called me 'young man' instead of my name."

Tiffany smiled.

"The first time I took care of a female patient and washed her, it unnerved me." His fingers traced the rim of his mug. "I had never seen an old woman naked before, and well, I was unprepared for the sight of her sagging breasts, flabby, hanging down toward her waist, the wrinkled skin on her abdomen."

"You bathed women as well as men?"

"Yes, but we respect the patient's dignity when we do it."

"How so?"

"We keep as much of the body covered as possible. As we wash each area—like the arm, leg, chest—only that part is visible while the rest of the body remains covered."

Tiffany nodded.

He frowned, rubbing his chin. "In the operating room half a dozen people may see patients naked, but if no one tells the patients about it, they'll never know."

Kite sighed. "When you die, your naked body lies on a cold stainless slab, exposed in front of strangers in a morgue or funeral home—until it's covered up. And there's nothing you can do about it."

Tiffany clutched the bottom of her cotton plaid shirt, leaving wrinkles as she unwound her fingers. "I never thought of it that way."

He pushed away his empty plate. "One time I walked a patient down the hall, a bit of exercise. Suddenly he grabbed my arm, retching, as he bent over to vomit."

"Where? In the hallway?"

"I didn't have anything close at hand, not even a wastebasket."

"Did you yell for help?"

"There wasn't time," said Kite.

"So what did you do?"

"I caught the vomit midstream."

Tiffany squealed and made a face. "How did you do it?"

"I cupped my hands," said Kite, holding his hands together, palms up, to demonstrate.

"I couldn't do it, not in a million years." She shook her head. For a moment, the hard glint in her eyes softened.

Kite pulled out the pen from his pocket. The one loaded with the chip to keep track of medications.

"What's this?"

"It's an injection pen, loaded with a microchip."

Tiffany frowned, looking at Kite warily.

"Yesterday, you became dizzy in the store, and I took you to see the doctor. You hadn't been taking your medication."

She opened her mouth to speak, but he cut her off.

"This is a prototype chip to track medications. Something I developed a while back, but it got put on the back burner."

"I've got my medication now. Don't need it."

"It'll help you to take your medication on time."

"How will it do that?"

"It will let us know when you've skipped, and when you're late."

"Oh, wait. It'll let *you* know?"

"Yes, both of us. And you'll never have to worry. I'll do all the worrying for you."

"How so?"

"I've programmed it to send out a reminder on your cell phone."

"This is kinda elaborate. Unnecessary, if you ask me."

"If you don't like it, I can take it out, anytime."

Tiffany stared at the pen, slowly shaking her head. "I don't know."

Kite pulled out the other pen, the one with the Number

9 chip. "I have something else. It will set the mood, make you feel better. Make love, not hate."

Tiffany looked from one pen to the other. "But they look the same to me. How do you tell them apart?"

Kite laughed. He pointed to a mark on the side of the Number 9 pen. "This is how I know." He held one in each hand. "Now which one will it be?"

THE END of Book 2

BOOK 3 OF THE ALTERATIONS TRILOGY

PRIMAL WILL

JANE SUEN

Chapter 1
DR. KITE

"SO, WHICH ONE WILL IT be?" Kite said, holding the two microchip injection pens, one in each hand. He offered them to her, a gift for his princess, as he had come to think of her.

Tiffany had heeded Lilly's warnings, expecting the worst in the man. She maintained her reserve and was on her guard. So far, Kite had been the perfect gentleman. The other day when she was dizzy and vulnerable, he took charge, making sure she got medical attention, remaining at her side. She had sensed—no, more than that—she *knew* he was interested in her, in more ways than just being friends.

She thought back to her last boyfriend. She had fallen crazy in love with him, his boyish charm, the way he tossed his hair to the side, his rebellious streak. He melted her reserves and took her on a roller coaster ride higher than she'd ever ridden. But, in the end, his immaturity broke her heart into bits and pieces, and she felt it would never be put back together again.

At this low point of her life, she found Lilly and enrolled in her program. Tiffany got through the pain, fought her way back, and started a new life. She graduated top in class. Kite had been her first assignment, a personal request from Lilly. She couldn't fail her.

Tiffany stared at Kite. He just stood there, not making a move to inject her, offering her a choice. She hesitated in the void of silence. *What will he do if she refused?* She exhaled, blowing a strand of hair away from her face.

Chapter 2

LILLY

SHE WAITED WITH A DEEPENING sense of dread and worry for Tiffany's call. The decision to assign her to Kite had been calculated, dependent upon Tiffany's graduation from the program, one of two women in the first class. Tiffany was capable, smart, and quick-witted. She had more street smarts than book smarts, unlike Naomi. Tiffany was someone Lilly trusted. Someone she trained. Lilly had been patient, waiting for the right person, the right time.

She swiped a finger across her cell phone, checking one more time for missed calls.

Naomi was as different from Tiffany as night was from day. The two women had met in the program and trained together. They complemented each other, pulling on the other's strength where one was weak in a way that made them better together than separate. They survived the program, rising to outdistance the others until only the two of them remained in the advanced class. They had become close, as friends and supporters, in this endeavor.

It didn't come as a surprise when Naomi volunteered to find Tiffany after numerous calls went unanswered.

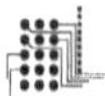

She picked up her cell phone and called.

"Naomi?"

"I'm in the car," said Naomi. Her voice was faint, surrounded by static and a hollow echo.

"Can you talk louder?" said Lilly, adjusting the volume, moving the phone closer to her ear.

"Yeah, I went to see Tiffany. I knocked on the door, but there was no answer." Naomi paused, steering the car down a narrow street. "She wasn't there. I looked in the windows and tried the door, but it was locked."

"Was her car there?"

"No."

"So where are you now?"

"Scouting the area. Looking for Tiffany."

"It's getting late."

"I'll stop soon to eat and find a place to stay tonight, then start back up in the morning."

"Did you check Kite's place?"

"The lights were all out."

"You be careful, okay?"

"Sure."

Chapter 3

ELLEN

To say she was nervous was an understatement. For months she had thought about Brad, throughout her pregnancy and after Angie was born. In moments of self-doubt over her impending role as a single mother, she had almost given in and reached out to Brad for help. But each time she had stopped before her fingers touched the phone.

She developed the rosy glow of pregnancy. Her baby became her first and most important priority. Gradually, the desire and connection to Brad diminished as the circumference of her belly increased.

She looked forward to the birth, as she'd made up her mind and resolved to be the best mom, to prove that she could do it. Ellen focused on this goal as the life inside her womb moved and kicked, exerting itself, extending a limb, exploring the boundaries of confinement.

Ellen tried to imagine what the baby would look like. Would she have the physique of her father, slim and muscular? Would the baby inherit the beauty of her mother?

Or would she carry Ellen's propensity for gaining weight and her fat cells? Would she have brains and beauty? Would she be healthy? She felt sure the baby would encompass the best of both parents. But she prayed, nevertheless, for this tiny life that she carried.

Ellen called her mother and father before she went to the hospital. When Angie was born, her mother was by her side, having gotten over the initial disappointment of Ellen having this baby without Brad.

Her mother had probed, tried to pry the details from Ellen. Ellen remained firm. Eventually, her mother stopped asking, knowing it was useless to push when Ellen had her mind made up. Mrs. Fulbright had raised Ellen to be an independent child. Finally, she'd let it go as her daughter came into motherhood on her own terms, and left Ellen to take this incredible journey without Brad.

As she gripped her mother's arm, beads of sweat gathered on Ellen's forehead. "Mom," she cried out, forcing the breath out in between the cramps that were coming closer and closer. Her doula was there, a young woman who had three children of her own.

"Push," the doula said.

Ellen nodded when it was time. Push she did, as hard as she could, again and again until the sound of crying erupted as the baby's tiny lungs released from her womb. She sank back on the pillow, exhausted, although she wanted to lean forward to catch the first glimpse of her baby, her Angie.

Someone fussed over her, fluffing her pillow, making her comfortable. In a brief moment, the nurse had measured and checked her baby, swaddling her in a blanket and placing a knit cap on her head, before laying her on Ellen's chest. She felt weak, the blood from her womb spotting the sheets as the nurse midwife sewed her back up.

The baby's heart pumped, pushing the blood through her arteries as Angie lay on top of her, right over Ellen's beating heart.

A knock at the door brought her back to the present. Ellen shifted Angie to her arm. When Angie was smaller, she had carried her in a sling. She chose it over the other baby carriers. It seemed like a perfect opportunity for mother-daughter bonding.

Now that Angie was a few months old, she held on, her legs clamping around Ellen's waist, tiny fists gripping Ellen's top.

"Angie, your dad's coming to see you," said Ellen.

She paused at the front door, turning to Angie. "You ready?" She planted a tender kiss on Angie's cheek before flinging the door open.

The clean-shaved, neatly dressed man at the door threw her a shy smile. He leaned in to greet her. "Ellen."

Ellen caught a whiff of his aftershave, his scent taking her back to the first time she met him, sitting next to her on the airplane. "Hi, Brad."

Last night Brad had tossed and turned in his bed, unable to sleep. The thought of meeting Angie for the first time, *his* daughter, the daughter he never knew he had, kept him awake for most the night. Between fits of sleep, he dreamed of her.

He crossed over the doorstep, looking at the baby in Ellen's arms, taking in her round chubby face, the long thick eyelashes framing her hazel eyes. "Angie," he said, as he beheld her dimpled arm and her tiny fingers. He held up a soft, stuffed puppy, the cutest one he could find with adorable eyes and big floppy ears.

Angie threw her head back and giggled at the sight of the toy, exposing the toothless gap in her little mouth.

His eyes lit up, relieved at her response. Brad let go of his fears and worries, and joined his daughter with boisterous laughter of his own.

Chapter 4
GIGI

REX PICKED UP THE PHONE and called Steve Cosine. He had been surprised to hear from him. Last he'd heard, they had run into dead ends on the investigation of Gigi's accident. Now, the match on the fingerprints taken from the van used to transport Gigi to Hotel Seven sounded crucial and perhaps the missing link to discovering who was responsible.

"I've been expecting your call," said Steve, picking up on the first ring.

"We got your email. It sounded like you have an important breakthrough."

"I've been working with the detective assigned to her case. Although it's been simmering on the back burner."

"Heavy workload?"

"Our caseload exploded since the storm."

"I can imagine," said Rex, sympathetically.

"How's Gigi, by the way?"

"Gigi is good. The nightmares are gone, and they haven't come back. We're on vacation at the moment, our first together."

"Does that mean you're in a relationship now?"

"Happily as a couple," said Rex.

"Give her my best," said Steve. "Rex, when are you guys coming back to the city?"

"We'll be back on Monday."

"Could you do me a favor?"

"Anything, old buddy."

"When you get home, would you and Gigi meet with me?"

"To talk about her case?"

"Yes, I'd like to see you both, and I have some questions for her."

"I'm not sure she can shed more light on what happened that day," said Rex. "You know she was pretty shaken up after the car accident."

"I just need to sit down and talk to her. The match on the fingerprints is our big break, but there are still some missing pieces of information."

"I'll see what we can do, since it's that important."

"Hold on. I'm checking my schedule for the first of next week," said Steve. "I have some openings Monday afternoon at 3:00 p.m. and in the early evening."

"Can you come by our place? We'll be getting home just after lunch, and that'll give us some time to unpack."

"Sure, and, oh Rex?"

"What?"

"I'm happy for you, man."

Rex sported a grin as he ended the call, glad to be hearing from his old buddy and anticipating more good news when they meet.

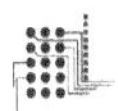

One thing about Steve was his excellent reputation with the police force, which carried through when he retired and became a consultant. Relentless. Persistent. His *modus operandi.*

In the aftermath of the storm that wreaked havoc in the city, Steve had been in demand. He didn't hesitate to jump in and help when they called him. In addition to his police work, his experience in insurance was a plus. His buddies on the force were all too glad to see him back. They were stretched thin, working around the clock. He was assigned to the vehicle recovery unit.

He worked his way down the vast list, compiled painstakingly from multiple sources of information. Each vehicle tracked down, and the owners notified. Sometimes they'd hit a stumbling block if the owner moved and the contact information on the registration was no longer current. Finding the owner took ingenuity and hard work, but it was the kind that Steve enjoyed. That, and sometimes strokes of pure luck. It was one of those days when he picked up the file on the white van, abandoned close to a warehouse that burned. Flipping through it, a name caught his eye. Raul.

Where had he seen that name? He rubbed his forehead, bent low over the paperwork. He was tired. So many cases, so few hours. Something about the name clicked. White van. He stared at the name, typed neatly on the paper, surrounded by white space. With a sigh, he closed the file and put it on top of his pile. He'd sleep on it and come back to it in the morning.

That night, Steve stopped by his favorite diner on the way home. He grabbed a quick bite since it was already past nine. Tomorrow Steve would be tired again if he didn't get more sleep and back on schedule.

Steve knew the route, it was the same one he'd taken for more than twenty years. The one that he knew by heart, every turn, dip, and corner. His mind wandered. The monotony of the road blending with the last rays of sunlight.

His headlights came on automatically. Unbidden, the thought came to him, the one that put two and two together. Bingo. He was staring at the face of Raul now, the man he'd visited after Gigi's car accident, the one whose white van had been stolen, the one with an expired registration.

In possession of the vehicle, he had taken fingerprints and sent it off to check for a match. Could this be the same van used to transport Gigi to Hotel Seven?

Steve was a patient man. He didn't like unsolved cases. Through his contacts on the force, the fingerprints from the white van got expedited processing. It got a match—to a dead man.

Chapter 5
DR. KITE

Tiffany waited for Kite's explanation. She wanted him to tell her. Lilly's warning had been loud and clear. Kite finally made his move and it was a big one. *Would he do something against her will? Would he hurt her?*

She searched his face for clues. Watched his body language, trying to get a read. She closed her eyes and counted silently to three. When she opened them, Kite was frowning at her.

"Tiffany, are you all right?"

She held up her hand.

"Maybe you should sit down, if you're feeling dizzy."

She nodded, moving to the couch.

Kite opened his palm, displaying the pen. "This is a mini-syringe filled with a medication-tracking microchip. Injection is quick and painless, a tiny pinch like a mosquito bite. With a reminder programmed, the chip will send you an alert to take your meds."

"A reminder?"

"Yes, it'll be sent to your mobile device. I'll also get it."

"But, you know I didn't take my meds because I didn't have enough money. It wasn't because I forgot."

"It works the same in either case. The bottom line is to get you to take your meds when you've missed it."

She sighed, gesturing to Kite's other hand. "What about that one? What do you have here?"

Kite stiffened, sucking in a deep breath. "This is a prototype chip I'd been working on—you know my story, the storm, the fire destroying the warehouse."

She nodded.

"I thought I'd lost it all, but fortunately I had these two microchips with me, tucked in the inner pockets of my laptop bag." He paused. "This chip is pheromone-specific, a love potion, as some would say."

"Specific?"

"Yes, to the pheromones it detects at the time of injection."

"Why would I need that?"

"Um . . . it'll enhance pheromones."

"I don't see how that would help me," said Tiffany.

"Think about it. Then ask me any questions you have," said Kite vaguely.

"What if I change my mind, decide I don't want it?"

"That's simple; I'll remove it from your arm."

Tiffany knew that the moment had come. Lilly had warned her that Kite might try this. All the months of their planning came down to this. The decision rested with her.

Chapter 6
ELLEN

MONDAY MORNING, WHEN SHE ARRIVED at work, Ellen saw a folded note taped on her door. Snatching it off, she read, *Please see me. Andrew*

An involuntary shiver quaked through her body. Ellen entered her office, plopped down her briefcase, and sat. Just for a moment. She needed a few minutes to regroup, to think. Her mind ran wild. This special summons caught her by surprise. Andrew. So formal. Foreboding. What happened to his insistence that she call him Andy? Had she done something wrong?

Dreading the meeting, she snaked her way to the break room, hoping someone had made coffee. Thankfully, someone had left half a pot of the morning brew. She poured, filling her favorite green ceramic mug. Taking her cup of joe black today, she inhaled the aroma, eyes closed for the full experience, before swallowing a big gulp. Ellen dropped off the mug in her office on her way to see Andrew.

A knock on his door elicited an immediate, "Come in." Andrew was expecting her.

Putting on a cheerful face, Ellen entered. "Good morning." She left off her usual 'Andy' to be safe. Perhaps he preferred Andrew now?

Andy was sitting straight in his chair, arms crossed.

She held up his note. "I got your note."

He nodded, gesturing her to come closer.

"You wanted to see me?" She left out asking, *What's wrong?* The question was burning in her mind.

"Have a seat." He waited until she sat, prolonging the tension. "Is there something you'd like to tell me?"

"I . . . I don't understand," said Ellen, stuttering.

"You left suddenly during the social hosted by Ergon Towers."

Ellen raised her eyebrows, wondering what Andy was going to say next.

"I was worried all weekend. Is something wrong?"

Ellen breathed a silent sigh of relief. She thought she'd mucked up his big project, or worse. She shook her head. "I didn't mean to worry you. I'm sorry."

"Are you okay?"

She nodded. "Yes, I'm fine."

His clenched jaws relaxed a bit. "Are you mad at me?"

Ellen's mind took a sharp turn. So this was why! "Not at all. I'm sorry if I gave that wrong impression. You know I couldn't party all night like the rest of you."

He persisted. "You didn't say goodbye. You just left all of a sudden."

She gave a forced laugh. "I had to look in on Angie. She hasn't been feeling well." She added the fib about Angie, the words tumbling out before she could put a stop to it. Ellen didn't usually lie and hated doing so, but this came under extreme circumstances. Besides, she reasoned with herself; it *was* about Angie and her father. Her protective mother's instinct came out in full force. Ellen wasn't going to tell him about Brad. It was *none* of his business.

Chapter 7

LILLY

SHE CHEWED HER LIP, THINKING about Tiffany. Sending Naomi may not have been the best move, but it was the quickest. Tiffany had been unreachable. If she needed help, Naomi would be reliable.

Lilly recalled the first day she met them. If she had to guess then, she would have been wrong. Tiffany was a mess, emotionally, coming fresh from a relationship break-up. The headiest drug wasn't some powder or pill; it was love, more powerful than anything you can buy or get. And Naomi, she was the opposite. Tight, buttoned up, a hard nut to crack. She didn't show her emotions. She came with baggage too. They all did.

The program attracted people who needed a fresh start. The first part took two weeks. It was grueling. A process to cleanse the body of toxins and waste products, and a sharpening of the conscious mind to the realm of the unconscious. It was taxing physically and mentally. Only those who were determined to finish made it to the end. The ones who dropped out; they just weren't ready. They were looking for hand-holding, sympathy, anything other than what the program required, and not prepared to do the hard work. But for those that did make it through, the end was satisfying.

Lilly had offered the second part of the program to the five women who finished. Three of the five weren't interested. These women had achieved what they came for, got what they needed, and they were ready to go back.

Picking up the calendar, Lilly stared at the date circled. In three days, it would be the end of the program. If she could leave now, she would. But she couldn't, not before it ended. The wait was going to be torture. Working quickly, she mapped out a new plan, one she'd see to herself. One she'd looked forward to with long-awaited anticipation and dreaded at the same time.

Chapter 8
DR. KITE

Kite didn't want to push her. He had never forced anyone, except for the ones who were incoherent, too drunk or high, or passed out—the ones the fake taxicab trawling the city at night picked up and brought to the warehouse. Kite wasn't proud of that, what he did. He rationalized away his guilt. He gave them a microchip, a night's sleep, and released them the next morning. In the name of science, he created novel technologies to cure illnesses, reverse aging, lose weight, and uplift moods.

As much as he wanted to inject Tiffany, he held back, giving her the time to decide. He just wanted to help her, right? Oh, right. He had his selfish motives. Tiffany was different, not like anyone he'd met. She was more than a guinea pig; he wrestled with his thoughts, his feelings. She was the one who brought him out of the utter depths he had sunk into after the warehouse burned to the ground. Even if he had any, Kite wouldn't have given her the mind-control chips, a problem since two out of three of the chips he'd implanted were defective.

"Hey, are you off in another world?" said Tiffany, touching his arm.

He shook his head, focusing on her.

"Talk to me, tell me more about the chips."

"You know what happened to the warehouse?" said Kite.

She nodded.

"We had trawled the city at night, picking up people drunk or high, passed out on the sidewalk. They got injected with a microchip and spent the night there sleeping."

"Did you get consent before you injected them with the chip?"

Kite looked down, uncomfortable. "No, they were incoherent, too far gone, out of it." He paused. "I violated the ethics of human experimentation."

"You didn't give them a choice."

"They didn't even know."

The confession of his wrongdoing hung heavy in the air.

Tiffany broke the silence. "So, what happened next?"

"The next morning, we released them."

"And the fire?"

"Destroyed the warehouse—"

"What happened to the people?"

"Nobody died in the fire, because it happened later in the day after we'd released all of them."

Tiffany sighed with relief. She had dreaded asking the question and finding out the answer. She knew she had to earn his trust before he'd tell her the truth. *Could she have faced the man if he was a murderer, had blood on his hands?* This part of the assignment had been eating at her, one that made her sick to the stomach, one she wasn't sure she'd have the strength to deal with, had it come to that.

The other part of her assignment was to find out about the microchips.

"And your chips?"

"Burned in the fire."

"All of them?"

"All except the two that I have here. These are prototypes of two other types of chips. I had put them aside to work on the new mind-control chips instead."

"And you just found them?"

Kite nodded.

Tiffany looked into Kite's eyes. She saw truth, sincerity, and something else—a deliverance from the pain, guilt, and load he'd been carrying.

Chapter 9
GIGI

"LET'S DO SOMETHING SPECIAL TODAY," said Gigi, turning to Rex. Sipping coffee at the kitchen counter, thinking they would be leaving tomorrow, brought a pang of sadness.

He nodded, knowing her well, and what she was thinking. How did nine days fly by so quickly? He tried not to dwell on the inevitable, to enjoy their remaining time together in this beautiful place.

"I remember picking up some pamphlets on a trip to town to get groceries, and I stuck them in the kitchen drawer." He got up to retrieve them, bringing them back to Gigi and spreading them on the counter. He scanned them now, stopping at one picture. A working ranch, one that advertised rides. Maybe Gigi would be interested. He pointed to it. "Have you ever ridden a horse?"

Gigi's eyes opened wide. "Me, ride a horse?" She was a city girl and had never been out to a ranch. The closest thing she got to horses was watching TV.

Rex smiled. He'd love to see this. "Why not try it? You're

the one who said you wanted to do something special today."

She picked up the pamphlet, turning it over to study the pictures and read the descriptions before making up her mind. "Okay, let's do it."

A quick call secured a reservation at the corral for the horseback riding lessons. Rex also got directions to the place.

"The owner said we could arrive earlier if we want to tour the ranch, feed the chickens, and see the animals. Do you want to do that?"

"Yes, that sounds fun."

Rex did a quick calculation in his head. "If we leave now, we'll have time to stop in town to pick up a picnic lunch, then head out to the ranch."

"Ooh," squealed Gigi, barely able to contain her excitement. "And a picnic lunch . . . yeah!" She reached over to hug Rex and planted a firm smooch on his lips.

He closed his eyes, enjoying Gigi's kiss, her sweet, soft, tender lips. He was conscious of her energy radiating through her body. Gigi's enthusiasm was infectious. He felt it. His body craved it. Man, he was happy. He kissed her back, wanting more of it. More of her.

There were five horses in the corral. The trainer picked one for Gigi, the black one, Lucy. He saddled her, and the brown one for Rex, and one for himself.

As Gigi sauntered up to Lucy, the horse turned its head,

watching her. She could smell the horses now, the muck from the stables. Up close, Gigi came eye-to-eye with Lucy. Her large brown eyes and long lashes, the wind-blown mane between pointed ears.

Lucy shook her head and snorted. Her nostrils flared, the size of small pancakes, moist and soft.

Gigi jumped back, aware of how close they were, keeping her hands down as she didn't want to spook Lucy.

Rex stood beside her, giving her encouragement. "Let her check you out."

Gigi smiled nervously. "She's magnificent. So big and tall, I can't see over her."

"You'll be fine."

The trainer stepped forward. "First-timer?"

Gigi nodded eagerly.

"Let's get you up. Put your foot in the stirrup. I'll help you."

"Will she move?" asked Gigi, eyeing the saddle warily, in awe of Lucy's spectacular muscular back and long thin legs.

"Lucy is gentle and patient," said the trainer as he held the reins, giving Gigi the instructions. "I'll be riding beside you if you need me."

After a few tries Gigi was finally hoisted into the saddle, mounted and ready to go. Sitting on top of Lucy, she felt ten feet tall. As Lucy started to move, Gigi panicked for a moment. She gripped the reins tightly and turned to look at Rex.

Rex grinned as he nodded reassuringly. "Take it easy on the reins. Go slow. I'm right here."

Rex watched her, the stiffness of an inexperienced rider apparent, thinking she ought to lighten up. "Hey, I think she likes you."

"Really?" said Gigi, breaking into a smile as she looked down at Lucy. Gigi cooed, "Oh, Lucy." She called out Lucy's name several times, sure Lucy's her ears perked up with "I luva you."

"You're gonna talk baby-talk to a horse?" Rex pretended to be shocked.

Gigi laughed at his horrified expression.

Rex thought, *it's good to see her laugh, to have a break from her intense concentration.*

Soon Gigi was talking and singing to Lucy, almost nonstop because Lucy couldn't talk back.

It was hilarious, those two, thought Rex as he watched Gigi bounce in the saddle. He was pleased with how relaxed she had become once she got over her initial fear and nervousness.

"I miss riding horses. But you know, it's like riding a bicycle. Once you learn, you won't forget," said Rex.

"I love Lucy," said Gigi, laughing. She felt alive, invigorated. Rex knew her so well, knew what Gigi needed, knew it before she knew herself. How could she have doubted him? Shortchanged him? A swell of affection filled her heart as she turned and looked at him, a lump in her throat. Today was their last day in paradise. They weren't galloping away into the sunset, but this was even better.

Rex snapped a photo.

Smiling, she urged Lucy forward.

Chapter 10

ELLEN

HUMP DAY. FINALLY, MID-WEEK ROLLED around. It was too slow, in Ellen's opinion. She glanced at the time on her cell. Another thirty minutes and she'd be out of there. She went back to her stack of papers, staring at the same page. Her mind wandered elsewhere, willing the time to go faster.

The knock on the door made her jump. It announced an unwelcome intrusion. Too late to put on her coat and escape. The door opened before she could invite them in. Only one person would do that.

"What are you working on?"

She looked up, hoping he wouldn't notice how tense she was. "Going over the preliminary reports for our meeting."

"Show me. Let's look over it now," said Andy as he closed the door.

"I don't think that's a good idea, Andy," said Ellen. "I have some more work to do. Will tomorrow morning work?" Ellen stared at him, taking notice of his pressed lips, the slight hint of anger. At her. She wasn't expecting this.

He hadn't given her a deadline.

"What?" snapped Andy as he took a step closer.

"I mean, with all due respect, please let me finish up and fix any errors," said Ellen, lowering her voice until it was barely audible, hoping it would soothe him. "Before wasting your valuable time on it." She didn't need this today. Today was one of the days she *had* to leave on time. Her mother had agreed to take care of Angie, having assumed Ellen had to work late. Ellen let it go at that, for now. She didn't go into the real reason—meeting Brad after work.

Andy stopped, blinking, trying to decide.

Ellen could feel her heart thumping, the beat pulsing through her body. She uttered a silent prayer. Please, please. What had gotten into Andy? This Jekyll and Hyde aspect of his personality was a new reveal. The charming man, the old Andy, was gone. In front of her was a different Andy, one that she didn't know and didn't like. She faked a smile, the most beguiling one she could muster. "I'll have it finished for you tonight. First thing in the morning I'll meet with you."

He stood, glaring at her.

"I'm so sorry I didn't meet your expectations. Please give me a chance."

"Send me the report tonight," said Andy, briskly. His anger and irritation still brewing, although somewhat abated with her apology.

"I'll email it to you," said Ellen, pushing the feeling of dread down, as if she didn't have enough to do tonight, and knowing she'd be spending a sleepless night.

Just as abruptly, he turned and walked out the door. Ellen glanced at the time. It was two minutes after five o'clock.

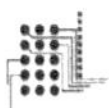

Driving through the rush hour traffic, Ellen breathed a sigh of relief. She wanted to put the unpleasant encounter behind her, not let it spoil the evening. She was meeting Brad for dinner, then expecting to make it home by early evening.

She smiled, her thoughts wandering back to Sunday when Brad came to her house to meet Angie. The next day he had called her, asking if she had time to grab a quick bite after work on Wednesday. He kept his tone neutral, not betraying his thoughts except to say Angie was a beautiful baby.

The diner was on her way home, a convenient stop for both of them. Its menu featured American cuisine, capitalizing on the words 'home-cooked' and 'made from scratch.' Ellen pulled into the parking lot. Getting out from her car, she saw Brad wave, sitting at a table by the window.

Brad rose to his feet, smiling to greet her as she walked in, pulling a chair out.

Ellen sat, grateful for Brad's chivalry, for this change in scenery. A solitary plucked flower in a small glass vase graced the table. The flatware came wrapped in a paper napkin, delivering the promise of an unadorned set and a plain meal. Her glass had water in it, filled with ice. A menu lay next to it. She smiled back.

"Glad you could make it," said Brad.

"Me too," said Ellen, thinking, *you have no idea.*

"Have you eaten here?"

Ellen shook her head. "I've passed by it, but never stopped." She scanned the menu. "Is the food good?"

"If you like a simple meal, the old-fashioned, home-cooked kind."

The waitress appeared. After a quick greeting, she went straight to business. "What'll you have?"

"How's your special today?"

"It's selling out like hotcakes."

I'll have it," said Brad, pushing the menu to her.

She turned to Ellen, showing the name "Maddy" pinned on her blouse.

"Let me have your fish and fries."

"Can't go wrong with that," said Maddy approvingly as she picked up the menus and left.

"Good day today?" said Brad.

"It could have been better," said Ellen, deciding not to get into it. "How's yours?"

"Busy, and productive. I didn't eat lunch today."

"Ooh, do you have a cafeteria?"

"We do, but it closes early. If you miss the hot food, then it's snacks from the vending machine."

"I take it you don't cook and bring your lunch?"

"Are you kidding?" said Brad, laughing. Then he straightened up and turned serious. "I *can* boil an egg."

"Mind telling me how long you boil them?"

"I set my timer to twenty minutes," said Brad in all

earnest. It was the one thing he knew how to do in the kitchen, and he was proud of it.

"You must like your yolks rock solid," said Ellen, a mischievous grin spreading as she teased him.

"Oh yes," he replied solemnly, not catching her drift.

"Well, I boil my eggs for eight minutes, nine minutes tops. You know if you cook them too long, the egg whites will start to get rubbery and the yolk hard," said Ellen.

"You like them soft, and I like them hard—just like they call them—hard-boiled eggs," said Brad, beaming.

"You know there's more than one way to boil an egg?"

"Just saying, if you ever boil them for me, that's how *I* like them."

"Is that an invitation for breakfast?" said Ellen playfully, feeling a strong urge to boil an egg and slowly peel it for him, stripping away the shell bit by bit.

As they chatted, Ellen relaxed in her chair, enjoying the unpretentious hospitality of the place until the meal arrived. Watching Brad dive into his food, seeing how hungry he was, she waited until he had finished before asking, "So Brad, what was it you wanted to talk to me about?"

"Angie," said Brad. "How adorable she is, and you—"

"She's the love of my life. I couldn't be happier."

"I see that. You've done a great job."

Ellen beamed, hearing him gush over her baby. *Their baby.*

"I've been thinking," said Brad. He wiped his mouth with the napkin, then paused to hold her gaze for a moment. "And I don't want you to take it the wrong way." He swallowed, starting over. "I've been thinking about all this, the shock of finding out that I have a daughter, meeting her for the first time, falling in love with her too—"

Ellen nodded.

"I never thought I'd be a father. I was immersed in my career, traveling a lot, and the last thing on my mind was a baby." He drew in a long breath. "When I met you, we had a lot of fun. After you stopped answering my calls, texts, and even the door, I thought that was it. That you didn't want to see me anymore. I had no idea of the real reason."

"I'm sorry to put you through that," said Ellen. "I had to wrestle with it, figure things out. Then, when I decided to go ahead with the pregnancy and keep Angie, I was determined to do it on my own, to become the best mother I could."

"I'm starting to understand that. Meeting Angie has changed my life too." His fingers played with a spoon. "That's what I want to talk to you about." He pushed the spoon away and sat up, meeting her gaze directly. "I want to be part of Angie's life. I wanted to talk to you and see how we can work it out."

Ellen had held her breath, waiting for him to tell her, not sure what he'd say. As she listened to him, she felt warmth expand in the pit of her stomach. She closed her eyes, holding that moment to herself.

"Ellen," said Brad, gently prodding her back to the conversation.

"Baby steps, okay?"

"Yes, one step at a time," said Brad, liking where this was going, looking forward to taking the first step.

"Oh, Brad," said Ellen. "Angie will be six months old next week."

"Her birthday is on the eleventh, right?"

"How about . . ." said Ellen, as an idea started to form, "a little celebration on her six month birthday?"

"Oh, I like that," said Brad, getting excited.

"A little party with cake and ice cream?"

"And presents."

"What about guests? I could invite my mom and dad," said Ellen.

"Mine live out of town, but I will invite them."

"You've told them?"

"Yeah, they were thrilled. My parents asked for a picture of Angie."

"Yes, of course," said Ellen, delighted. "Would they like a framed photo or digital?"

"Either is fine, or both. And I'd like one for myself too."

"Do they like to travel?"

"They are getting on in age and not traveling as much."

"We'll just have a little party this time, then maybe plan for a big one-year celebration?"

"They can't wait to see their first grandchild. I'm sure they would be delighted."

The ideas were churning as they discussed and made plans, and it felt so good to Ellen. So good that she almost forgot the time, that she had to go.

Chapter 11

LILLY

LILLY KICKED HER SHOES OFF at the door and flung her purse on the table. Barefoot, she walked to the kitchen and grabbed a spritzer from the refrigerator. This day hadn't gone well, and she couldn't wait to get home.

The knock on the door broke the silence. Lilly swiveled, caught by surprise. Who could it be? She wasn't expecting anyone. As if the day could get any worse; now wasn't the time to talk to anyone. She hesitated. The knock persisted, louder this time. Sighing, she opened the door to find a tall, good-looking man with a rugged face standing outside.

"Hello, Mrs. Cooper."

She froze, staring at the same man who had come to question her about Gary, the cab driver who was found dead on the sidewalk outside her home. She was surprised to see him again.

"Do you remember me, Mrs. Cooper?"

"I didn't catch your name—"

"Steve Cosine." He paused politely. "Do you have a few minutes to talk?"

"Now's not a good time."

"This won't take long," said Steve, taking a step forward to look over her shoulder.

"I just got home."

"A few minutes and I'll be out of your hair."

"I've already answered your questions before," said Lilly, irritated.

"If you'll allow me," said Steve in his smooth, deep voice.

Lilly shrugged, resigned to get this over as quickly as possible. She gestured, pointing to the wooden chair in the living room, while she moved to sit on the couch. "What's this about?"

"I have some questions for you about Gary Smith who drove a cab. He was found dead in front of your home the day of the big storm."

"We've already gone over that," snapped Lilly.

"I have a few more. Have you ever been to the warehouse at Peter's Street?"

"No, I don't know the place." Lilly frowned. "What does this have to do with me?"

"We found Gary's fingerprints on a van parked outside the warehouse," said Steve, eyes probing Lilly.

Lilly shook her head.

Steve shifted in his chair. "We traced the warehouse to a Dr. Kite. Do you know him?"

"Kite—" said Lilly, as she stiffened, clenching her jaw. It wasn't the direction she wanted to take.

"Please answer my questions. We have reason to believe Kite is missing, and he may be another link to Gary."

"I'm afraid I can't help you." She stifled a cry, frozen in fear at the mention of Gary's name as it brought back visions of his death, and the reason Steve came to her home to question her that first time.

"Can't—or won't?" said Steve, eyes piercing.

Lilly rubbed her knee, trying to stall, biding her time.

"I ran a check on Kite's credit cards—when he used them, where he went," said Steve. "All activity stopped the day after the storm."

Lilly licked her lips.

"I'm going to ask you again. I advise you to think hard about Kite."

She sighed and spread her hands on her thighs. "Now that I think about it, I did meet Kite, but it was briefly at a restaurant."

"Would that have been at Duggers?"

A sinking feeling came over Lilly as she realized that Steve knew more than she had guessed.

"I met him there once, but it was by accident."

"So you didn't know this Kite before that?"

"No."

"How did this, umm, accident come about?"

"I had already finished the main course when he arrived. I had taken his lucky table, but of course, I had no way of knowing. So when the hostess brought him to his usual table—the table I was sitting at—he was disappointed to see it occupied."

"Then what happened?"

"I invited him to sit with me while I had my dessert."

"Didn't you think it was odd?"

She shook her head. "No. It was a chance meeting, his lucky day, as he said." She added, "He turned out to be a pleasant table companion, gracious and grateful for the kindness."

"And yours? Was it also your lucky day?"

"At the time it felt like it."

Chapter 12

DR. KITE

WATCHING TIFFANY LEAVE, GET IN her car and drive away, Kite felt let down, his enthusiasm dampened. He felt sure Tiffany was stalling. Kite didn't know why. Still, he was willing to give her some more time to think about it, to make a choice.

He had the two chips left, and that was all he had to offer her. Kite had almost no money, and no wish to continue the trawling for human test subjects. That part of his life seemed a distant past. The shock and trauma of the fire, seeing the blackened remains of his warehouse smoldering under the embers, hastened Kite's decision to close that chapter in his life.

He clenched his fist, gripping it hard. Cursing. It wasn't how things should have turned out, what he had envisioned in his mind. A fantasy, a happily ever after, had slipped between his fingers. How could he have been so wrong? What was he thinking?

She didn't know where she was going. Tiffany drove aimlessly, on autopilot. Her mind was elsewhere. Overhead, the clouds gathered, drawing a curtain over the day, summoning the night before its time.

It wasn't supposed to be like this. For several months, Tiffany had played the part dutifully, going along with the plan. Kite was a subject, an assignment. No more, no less. She'd let her objectivity slip a little at a time. A chipping away that she hadn't been aware of, or even wanted. She had to remind herself to remain focused, to stay the course, to keep her head on her shoulders. Was she going crazy?

Her car had a mind of its own, taking her down the coast to the pier. Dusk would soon be settling in, and this place was her favorite on the beach. A little pier, now fallen into disuse, the wood on the far end slowly rotting in the water. No longer safe, it still commanded a majestic sight, a runway rising above the water and held up by crisscrosses of thick, long wooden poles.

She could feel the dampness in the air as moisture seeped into her clothes and stuck to her skin. She turned to watch the sunset. The crisp color veiled by the clouds.

Tiffany could smell the ocean, the swell from afar carrying all sorts of sea creatures and shells spilled onto the beach. She could hear the waves, powerful and rhythmic.

The cry of seagulls flying overhead broke the serenity of the moment.

It was a place she escaped to when she wanted to be by herself. One that asked nothing and took nothing. She found peace and acceptance here. She was just a blip in time, a dot on the beach. The vastness of the ocean, the endless stretches of sand, stirred a strong response. Had the beach been there, meeting the seas, for eons? She shivered as the darkness of the night descended, feeling her mortality, her fleeting existence on earth.

And Kite? She understood where his ego, vanity, and determination had taken him. And she glimpsed his remorse and humility.

Chapter 13

GIGI

Packing and leaving, Gigi felt a piece of her would always be there. And she carried with her the memories of the vacation, of Rex, the calm, peaceful feeling, the beauty of the land. Rex had suffered another relapse of his illness after the ranch outing, and he was struggling with his luggage. She walked over to him, placing an arm around his shoulders.

He turned, welcoming her gesture, her caring. "Hey girl," he said, smiling bravely to hide the pain.

"Let me get that," said Gigi as she lifted the suitcase into the trunk of their rental car. "Is this the last one?"

"Yup. Ready to go?" He paused, turning around one last time before leaving. "I'm going to miss this place."

She hooked her arm around his waist, feeling the curve of his hips. "Me too," said Gigi. She had been happy here in their hideaway. Gigi sighed, soon they would be back in the real world. She was worried about Rex. And anxious about what Steve Cosine had to say.

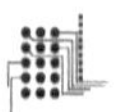

Steve dropped by their apartment Monday afternoon. He was dressed as usual in his frumpy shirt with no tie.

Rex clasped his friend's hand, delighted. "Man, it's good to see you."

Steve looked the same—tall and gangly, big bones that carried his frame effortlessly, the lined, weathered face still handsome. Add a hat and he'd easily pass for a cowboy.

"This retirement has been anything but quiet." He chuckled.

"You've been doing okay?"

"Yeah, exhausted is more like it. The unexpected havoc from the storm created a mess. A lot of cases since I've been recruited back to help." He ran his hand through his thick head of hair, reminded he needed to get it cut, although Steve was thankful he had the good hair genes, like his dad.

"Getting enough sleep?"

"About four to five hours."

"Man, that's not enough."

"It'll do. I don't have the luxury of sleeping longer."

"Hey, you're supposed to be retired. But it sounds like you're busier now than when you worked full-time."

Steve nodded. "The difference being I choose what I want to do, and how much I want to work."

"Would you like something to drink?" Rex headed to the kitchen.

"Sure, what've you got?"

Opening the refrigerator door, Rex pointed to the

bottled drinks. "We quit drinking beer. Got all kinds of juices and non-alcoholic drinks."

"I'll take a root beer," said Steve.

Rex nodded, grabbing a ginger zinger for himself.

They sat down at the kitchen table, waiting for Gigi to join them.

Rex wondered why she had disappeared so quickly after a quick hello to Steve when he'd arrived.

"Hey Gigi," Rex called. "We're in the kitchen. Are you coming?"

"Be there in a minute," said Gigi, as she changed into a comfortable T-shirt. She reached out to the dresser top, steadying herself. The unease Gigi felt since receiving the email from Steve crept back, bringing strong emotions and memories. She had suppressed them, put them out of sight and out of mind, and moved on with her life.

A thought crept up, casting a shadow over her. She shivered. Her secret. She had never told Rex. What if Steve had found out?

Chapter 14

ELLEN

"Angie asleep?" said Ellen as she stepped through her door.

Mrs. Fulbright put her two hands together and bent them, her head resting on top.

"I'm sorry, I ran a little late tonight."

"Problem?"

For once, Ellen didn't mind her mom's curious prying. A gnawing sense of dread, a discomfort. Now that she was home, the last thing she wanted to do was work on the report. The very last. But she had promised Andy.

"Here, come and sit with me," her mom said, patting the couch. "I can tell something is bothering you."

"Mom, Andy's gone weird on me."

"What do you mean?" She frowned. "I thought Andy's been sweet on you. I mean he's your boss, and he's an attractive man."

"He was, but he's changed."

"Changed? How so?"

Ellen gave a nervous laugh. "Like you wouldn't believe. I'm feeling it."

"Okay, now you're frightening me. When did this start?"

"The night of the social, he was charming, sexy, came on to me." She paused. "Then I met Brad and he wanted to talk, so we left the party. I told you about that."

Ellen's mom nodded.

"We went to an empty meeting room to talk." She frowned, trying to remember as she told the story. "We didn't close the door, but at one point in our discussion, I thought I heard something, a cough. I chalked it up to someone walking by in the hallway, although I didn't see anyone." Her hand flew to cover her mouth as her eyes opened wide. "Oh my God. Do you think Andy was lurking outside and listening to our conversation?"

"If he were watching you, he would've seen you leave . . ."

". . . with Brad, and he might have followed us . . ."

"When was the next time you talked to Andy?"

"On Monday morning. When I came to work, the first thing I saw was his short, terse note taped on my door."

"He wasn't in a good mood?"

"Not that day."

"Can you think of anything else that could have upset him that night, anything you said or did?"

Ellen shook her head.

"Then today he barged into my office right before I was getting ready to leave and gave me a hard time on the report that I was working on."

"Did you end up staying late to work?"

"I think that was his intention, but I stalled him, said I'd deliver the report to him tonight and see him first thing tomorrow morning."

Ellen straightened up, eyes sparkling as she clasped her hands. "Brad asked me to meet with him tonight," Ellen added quickly. "I've got exciting news to tell you."

Chapter 15

LILLY

SHE SPENT ANOTHER RESTLESS NIGHT, tossing and turning. Her plan with Kite wasn't going as smooth as she thought it'd go. She'd lived in fear of another knock on the door. Or rather a pounding at her door, one that could only mean one thing. The police were coming to get her.

The thought of spending time behind bars terrified her.

Tracking Kite down had been easier than anticipated. She was determined to find him. Lilly did the only thing she could do, and luck was on her side. She went back to Duggers, the restaurant where they met.

Lilly sat at his favorite table, his favorite place, and talked to the hostess. Sally was her name. She wasn't wrong. Old habits die hard. Before he left the city, Kite had his last meal there.

According to Sally, he stopped by to say goodbye to all his friends there.

"Did he say why he's leaving?" Lilly asked.

"Something about the storm and his business burned to the ground."

"Was he devastated?"

"Yeah, he was tearing up. He sat there, staring at his plate, slouched in his chair."

"Not his usual self, then."

"Oh no," said Sally, adamantly shaking her head. "I've never seen him like that."

"So he came by to say goodbye?"

"And have the last meal."

Lilly opened up to Sally. "I shared a table with Kite. Do you remember?"

"The only time that happened was a while ago. But that woman—" Sally looked puzzled for a moment. "She looked worn, torn up about something. And a lot older. I mean, that *couldn't* have been you."

Lilly smiled, nodding.

"What? But you look different now."

"Oh, that was the old me, and now you see the new me."

"Wow, I wouldn't have guessed. You, you're like a different person."

"Well, I cut my hair too."

"You sure did."

"Got rid of all my hair and the baggage with it," said Lilly. She leaned back. "And I feel so much lighter."

"Whatever you did, I want to know."

Lilly threw her head back and belted out a throaty laugh. "I want Kite to see me."

"Oh, he should see you. He won't even recognize you."

Lilly said quietly, "Look, I'm worried about Kite. Did he happen to mention where he's going?"

Sally whispered too, acting conspiratorial. "Well, he was headed toward the coast, a little town about twenty miles north of Chas Town."

"Ah, someplace quiet, away from the tourist crowd."

"I just know it's about a couple hours from here, two and a half max," said Sally. "A little hideaway mostly frequented by locals."

"You've been there?"

"A long time ago, as a child. We passed through there once. Stopped to have a meal at the diner." She smiled. "We ate at 'Square Meal.' Who can forget that name?"

Lilly paid for the meal and left a generous tip.

The waitress came back, assuming she wanted the change.

"No, you keep the change," said Lilly, smiling.

Chapter 16
GIGI

IF ANYONE WERE UP TO anything fishy, Steve would sniff it out. Sitting in the kitchen with Rex, waiting for Gigi, he thought she should be thrilled about the new lead in her case. *Why wasn't she? Did Gigi have something to hide?*

He got himself into this by doing a favor for Rex, helping him out. He glanced at Rex. He seemed entirely at ease, the same old Rex he'd always known. He checked the time. Eight minutes in the kitchen chatting with Rex and still no Gigi in sight.

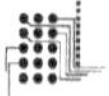

Putting her best face on, Gigi turned on her charm as she walked out to talk to Steve, offering a quick hug.

"You look great," said Steve, scanning her for signs of the accident or scars and finding none.

"So good to see you," said Gigi. "I never got to thank you in person for all that you did."

"No more nightmares?"

"All gone." Gigi smiled.

"Let me get to the point about the new development. You saw the email?"

Gigi nodded.

"The man that we traced the fingerprints to is dead," said Steve.

"Oh no," said Gigi.

"Unfortunately, he died in the storms."

"What was his name?"

"Gary."

"Was he driving the van?"

"When he died, he was driving a taxi."

"Uh . . . what's the connection with the taxi?"

Steve took a swig of his drink and put it down. "Let me explain. After the storm, the van was found parked in front of a warehouse that had burned."

"So Gary—"

"His prints were found on the van."

"So what's with the warehouse?" said Rex.

"We had to do some digging. We found a connection between the warehouse and a Dr. Kite."

"A medical doctor?" asked Rex.

"That is the puzzling part," said Steve, shaking his head. "This Kite, he didn't graduate from medical school or have a license to practice. But as far as we can tell, he was conducting some health-related research and experiments."

"So have you talked to this Kite?" said Rex.

"Not yet, but I have some leads I'm following up on."

Steve fiddled with his bottle, picking it up and turning it. He pretended to study the label as if the number of calories became of utmost importance.

"Gigi, help me understand the connection," said Steve. "The van, you, Gary, the warehouse."

She shook her head.

"Do you know this Gary?"

"No," said Gigi emphatically.

"What about Dr. Kite—Gigi, do you know him?" said Steve, eyeing her intently.

This question was one that Gigi dreaded. The secret she had kept from Rex. Gigi turned to look at him, throwing a smile to disarm any ill-feelings. She sat up, pulling her shoulders back.

"Yes," she whispered.

For a moment there was stunned silence in the room. Steve had toyed with the idea of a possible connection with Gigi, but to hear it was a different story.

Gigi reached over to touch Rex's hand. "I want to tell you something. But before I do, I want to apologize to you."

"I don't think you have to apologize."

"But I do, and I'm relieved to be doing this now," said Gigi. "I've been carrying this secret around."

Rex squeezed her hand.

She turned to him and paused. "I know Dr. Kite. He was my doctor."

Surprised, Rex stopped squeezing her hand.

"Remember when I had that condition, ringing and buzzing in my ears . . . the tinnitus?"

He nodded.

"It had gotten worse, constant, day and night. I couldn't deal with it, and I sought out doctors in search of some relief. I was frantic, out of options, and desperate. So when I heard about this doctor, who was unconventional and secretive, I became curious. The arrangement made was for me to be picked up by a cab driver and taken to see Kite. The first time I was blindfolded and didn't see where I was going."

"The first time? So you saw him more than once?"

"Yes."

"What happened?"

"He implanted a microchip in me," said Gigi. "It cured my illness."

"What kind of microchip?" said Rex. *How could Gigi have kept this from him?*

"It was a prototype, a new chip he had developed after years of research." She smiled. All I know is that he cured me of my disease, and he put me back to perfect working order."

"So can you talk about after that, when you went back the next time?" Steve asked.

"I hadn't thought of him for quite a while until he contacted me again."

"Was there a problem?"

"Not that I'm aware. Kite said he had received a new shipment, an upgraded mind-control microchip, and he wanted me to come in to have it replaced."

"How did you get there this time?"

"I was picked up by a cab driver the second time also."

"But you weren't blindfolded this time?" said Steve.

"This time, I saw where he took me."

Steve rapped the table with his hands. "Let me guess, the warehouse?"

Gigi nodded.

She sat back, relieved the truth had come out. She studied Rex's face to garner his response. She had seen confusion, which turned to anger. Now it was replaced by worried concern.

"Rex," said Gigi. "I'm sorry. Please forgive me. I never meant to keep secrets from you, but Kite swore me to secrecy before the first implant."

"Gigi, I had no idea you went through all this. I see you as a strong woman. And you kept your promise to Kite to keep it secret."

Steve said, "I have a few more questions." He pulled a photo from his pocket and laid it on the table. "This man." He tapped the face. "Do you know him, Gigi?"

She leaned in, studying his features. "Yes."

"Do you know his name?"

She shook her head.

"How do you know him then?"

"He was the cab driver. He took me to see Kite."

"Flip the photo over."

"Gary Smith," said Gigi, as she read the name written on the back.

Chapter 17

LILLY

NAOMI REPEATEDLY TRIED TO REACH Tiffany. Her previous calls had gone straight to voicemail. It was getting late, and she wanted to try once more before she called it a night.

On the second ring, Tiffany answered. "Hello?"

"Tiffany, I'm so glad I've finally reached you."

"Naomi?"

"Yeah, where have you been? I've been calling. I was worried something's happened to you."

"I took a walk on the beach. There's no cell service there."

"We must talk."

"Shoot, I'm listening."

"No, I mean in person. I'm *here*."

"What?" said Tiffany, surprised. "Why didn't you tell me you're coming?"

"Lilly sent me," said Naomi. "I dropped everything and scrambled to get here."

"Well, you shouldn't have."

"She was worried about you."

"Why, for Pete's sake?"

"Look, why don't we talk about it in person?" said Naomi. "I'm starved. Is there someplace we could grab a bite?"

Hearing a few low rumbles in her stomach, Tiffany was quick to respond. "Square Meal. You know where it is?"

"I passed by it earlier on my way into town."

"See you there in a few," said Tiffany.

The restaurant stood by itself on the edge of town. The faded wooden sign that said "Square Meal" had seen better days, the cracks in the paint a sad indicator of the disrepair. But it didn't seem to affect its customers, the local crowd that hung out, who trod on its worn floors and embraced the establishment despite its exterior decay.

Naomi was the first to arrive. At this late hour, a wide selection of tables was available. Catching sight of the waitress, she smiled. "Table for two, please."

The waitress nodded and waved her hand. "Hon, just sit anywhere you like."

Naomi slid across the bench seat to sit by the window.

She didn't have long to wait before the waitress came by with the menu and two sets of silverware laid on top of paper napkins. "What'll you have to drink?"

"How's your iced tea?"

"It's good, and not too sweet, if you know what I mean,"

said the waitress. "You know what you want to eat?"

Naomi shook her head. "I haven't decided yet." Looking up from the menu, she added, "My friend will be joining me."

"I'll be back with your drink."

Leaning against the hard back of the seat, Naomi took in the dim interior. An undefined color, some shade between gray and smoke-green, was painted over the washed-out interior. The dim light chased shadows and dark murky streaks on the wall.

"Thank you," said Naomi as the waitress set her drink on the table. Her eyes scanned the wood, marked with scratches, notches, and carved hearts bisected by arrows with initials inside. She wondered, how many couples have sat here carving their initials and they're still together? With her finger, she rubbed the heart in the center of the table, the biggest one she could see, feeling the ridges, following its curves and the crude initials.

"Hey, you made it," said Tiffany, interrupting Naomi's thoughts as she squeezed into the bench across from her.

Throwing her a warm smile, Naomi said, "I was close by."

The waitress appeared and took their order. The menu was sparse. They ordered quickly, and service was fast. Fried catfish and okra for Tiffany. Grilled shrimp and rice for Naomi.

"So how's the program going?"

"We're about to wrap up. Two more days until the end," said Naomi.

"Got some good prospects for round two?"

"Out of the twelve, in the beginning, we lost one. A handful made it this far to achieve a state of cleansing and renewal, both physically and mentally."

Tiffany nodded. "That sounds about right."

"Of course, they find out after they finish the program about the next round," said Naomi, with a slight frown. Lilly had demanded absolute hush on this, and she disagreed with it.

"And it's expected some will go home, having achieved the goals they signed up for," said Tiffany.

"And some will decide to go on as we did," added Naomi.

"Taking on assignments, changing the world one project at a time," said Tiffany, stifling a yawn.

"You got lucky on that one. I had to stay and help Lilly with the next class."

"You've got those superb organization skills," murmured Tiffany, smoothing things over. "Perfect for that job."

"Well, I'm here to help."

Tiffany quickly brought Naomi up to speed. When she got to the part about the two new microchips, Naomi's eyes widened.

"We need to tell Lilly. Have you talked to her?"

Tiffany shook her head. "Not yet."

"Let's do it now. Lilly's worried sick about you."

Tiffany picked up her cell phone and scrolled to Lilly's name.

Lilly picked up on the first ring.

"Hello."

"Naomi is here with me."

"Are you all right?"

"I'm fine. I turned my phone off when I met with Kite and was out of pocket for a while after that."

"So tell me what happened."

"He came to my apartment, you know, to check up on me."

"He was worried after your dizzy spell."

"Yes, and Kite brought groceries. I made coffee, and we chatted for awhile."

"Did you ask him about the warehouse?"

"It burned, everything was gone. But no one was hurt."

"And the chips?" said Lilly eagerly.

"He still has two microchips."

"Wait just a minute. So Kite's chips didn't all get destroyed in the fire?"

"Yes, but these weren't in the warehouse. Kite found them in his laptop carry bag."

"Go on."

"Well, he, um offered me a choice."

"A choice?"

"Between the two chips."

Lilly paused before continuing. "These chips, what do they do?"

"Well, one is a medication tracking chip, so you wouldn't forget to take meds like I did."

"And the other?"

"He mentioned pheromones, something like a love potion," said Tiffany as she looked at Naomi, catching her eye.

"Put Naomi on the phone, will you?"

She handed the cell over to Naomi, mouthing, "She wants to talk to you."

"I'm coming over there."

"But . . . the class isn't over yet."

"We've got two more days. Can you handle it?"

"So you want me to come back?"

"You know the drill."

Naomi gulped. Lilly must have a lot of faith in her to ask her to close the program. "Of course, Lilly."

"I knew I could count on you," said Lilly, relieved. "Oh, and hand the phone back to Tiffany please."

"You want to talk to me?" said Tiffany.

"Have you told Kite when you'd have a decision?"

"No, I just told him I needed time to think."

"Okay, call him and set up a time to meet tomorrow afternoon."

"But what about you?"

"I'll be there—but don't tell him yet."

"You're coming, right?"

"I should be arriving in the morning. I'll go straight to your apartment. See when Kite is available. Be sure to tell him to bring the microchips."

Chapter 18

ELLEN

Barely awake, Ellen dragged her heels getting ready for work. She stayed up way too late last night working on the report. But she finished and sent it in the early hours of the morning.

Suppressing a yawn as she got off the elevator, Ellen headed straight to her office. The door was ajar. Ellen was sure she had closed it the night before. Walking in, she saw a note taped to her computer. It was from Andy, telling her to see him—just like the one he wrote previously. How did he do it? Get here so early, beat her to the office—and he must've read her report. One thing Ellen was sure about that man, he was a workaholic.

She pulled a copy of the report from her briefcase and walked quickly to Andy's office. Better to get it over with—the sooner, the better. She took a second to compose herself, then knocked on his door firmly. She barely gave him time to respond before marching inside.

He met her at the door; he had been expecting her. This

morning he was back to his charming self. All smiles.

"Ellen," he said. His hand lingered on her arm, touching her bare skin as he guided her forward.

She jumped as a little spark of static electricity snapped between them.

"Ouch," said Andy, exaggerating. "That's quite a shock."

"I'm wide awake now."

"I see you stayed up all night."

"I was tired. I crashed on the couch."

"After you delivered the report," said Andy with a smirk.

"You've read it?"

"Sure did."

"So um, what do think?"

"It's good."

Ellen whirled, planning a quick escape.

"By the way, Ellen," said Andy.

Heart thumping, she slowly turned around.

"You need something else, boss?"

Quick as a fox, he moved, sliding up to her, so close his pant legs brushed hers.

She wriggled her foot a few inches away, hoping he wouldn't notice.

But he did. Closing in, Andy was now right on top of her.

Ellen could feel his breath blowing on her cheeks. No wiggle room left, he got her pinned.

Chapter 19

LILLY

She packed light, taking only a duffle bag for the trip. Time to get some sleep. She set her alarm for 5:00 a.m., plenty of time to drive to the coast and meet up with Tiffany. Soon she'd be face-to-face with Kite.

There was one more thing she had to do tonight. Whipping out her cell phone, she scrolled down the contacts list to find Steve Cosine.

Holding the phone to her ear, she got out a pad and scribbled a few words on it, as a reminder of what to say. The call went to voicemail. She left a message and asked Steve to call her that night, saying that it was urgent.

Chapter 20

DR. KITE

HE WALKED ALONG THE BEACH, hoping to calm his mind from the thoughts swirling around. He had to get away to think things through.

She said she needed time to think. Kite had stayed away, not calling her.

If Tiffany didn't respond by tomorrow, he was going to take matters into his own hands. He would, this time.

Taking his shoes off, Kite sunk his toes in the sand, feeling the coolness as he pushed his heels down. He stepped carefully, searching for seashells washed up on the beach from the Atlantic.

He kept his mind preoccupied, focusing on finding the one special shell buried amongst the abundant and common clams, cockles, and periwinkles.

His toe bumped into something. A knobby whelk. A few inches to the left of it, he glimpsed a scotch bonnet, his favorite. "Huh," grunted Kite, as he snatched it up. Blowing the sand off, he scraped the inside with his fingernail, scooping out embedded sand.

Occupied with finding seashells, he lost track of time. Leaving the beach, Kite checked his phone for the bars indicating cell coverage. This time she had called and left a voicemail.

His smile turned into a broad grin as he listened to her message. He wasted no time returning her call.

Chapter 21

LILLY

THE HARSH SOUND OF HER cell phone startled heavy-eyed Lilly from her slumber.

Cursing, she grabbed the phone.

"Hello," said Lilly, groggy from sleep.

"Oh, did I wake you up?" said Steve.

She didn't respond.

"I didn't hear your call earlier when I was in the shower," he continued smoothly.

She listened to the deep, masculine voice on the other end of the line, trying to picture the face of the caller.

"It's Steve Cosine, returning your call."

Oh crap! She clamped her hand over her mouth, glad he couldn't see her expression. "Oh, I did call you, didn't I?"

"Yes, ma'am," said Steve. "Is this too late to call you back?"

"No, tonight is fine." Lilly cleared her throat. "This is Lilly. You came to see me recently and gave me your card."

"Lilly Cooper," said Steve.

"You, um, said to call you if I had information about Dr. Kite."

"Have you heard from him?" asked Steve, his attention sharpened.

"Not exactly. But I found out where Kite is."

Stunned by this unexpected bit of news and Lilly's apparent willingness to work with him, he took out his notepad and a pen, ready to scribble.

"But before I tell you, I want you to promise that you won't do anything rash."

"I can't promise you anything, but I'll take it into consideration."

He could hear her let out a deep breath.

"I have a confession to make," said Lilly. The words slipped out past her lips somehow. Perhaps she felt easier talking to Steve over the phone. Maybe it was something about his voice that was soothing. Whatever the reason, she just wanted to tell him, to come clean. Now.

He waited for her to continue.

"When I met Kite, I was recently divorced. It left its mark on me, and I turned into a bitter, angry woman. That night at Duggers we talked friendly chit-chat at first. Later, before we left, he gave me his card."

"So you had another date?"

"Oh no, nothing of the sort."

"But you called him?" Steve prodded gently.

"Yes, about a medical procedure."

"I don't get it."

"I called and asked him to help me look and feel better,

to recover from the divorce."

"How would he do that?"

"His research. He had developed a prototype mind-control microchip for this. He offered it to me. I thought it over, made my decision, and called him back."

"Where's this chip?"

"He injected it in me."

A chip, inside Lilly. He whistled, letting it sink in—what Lilly just said, and what Gigi said.

"It's in you now?"

"In my arm."

"So you have news about Kite?" said Steve.

"Yes, and I've found him—finally."

"Where?"

"In a little town about twenty miles north of Chas Town."

"That's not too far from here."

"I'm heading out there in the morning," said Lilly, yawning. "That's why I went to sleep early."

Steve thought hard. Things were moving fast now, the pieces all of a sudden falling in place. The van, Gary, the warehouse. Kite, Gigi, Lilly.

"When are you leaving?"

"Five o'clock," said Lilly, adding abruptly, "Look, I've got to go or I'm not going to be able to get up early."

"I'm coming with you," said Steve.

Chapter 22

ELLEN

HER LIPSTICK WAS SMEARED. A few strands of hair slipped out from her neat bun. Ellen stared in the bathroom mirror as she let the water run from the faucet. Grabbing a towel and wetting it, she poured soap on it before scrubbing her lips, then her face clean. Devoid of makeup, she got another towel and repeated the same procedure.

Making her way to a stall, she went in and locked the door. Alone, safe, she closed her eyes as she leaned back.

What was he thinking? She had said no. That didn't stop Andy from coming up close, pressing against her, his thighs moving and touching hers, his breath warm on her cheek.

Ellen felt trapped, pinned next to the wall. They were in his office. She didn't dare scream, yet she wanted to. Up close, his attractive face turned ugly. Insistent. She didn't want this. It was all wrong.

Stunned, she froze. Like a frightened rabbit. Her mind trying to process what was happening. To her. In Andy's office.

Then he rubbed on her, his breathing becoming faster.

She wriggled her arm up in front of her chest, wedging a space between them.

With a quick movement, he flung her arm out, his fingernails digging into her, hurting her.

She cried out, "No!"

It angered him. He grabbed Ellen's cheeks and forced her head back, pushing his lips down on hers.

She turned her head, squirming.

It was the loud knock on his office door that saved her.

Chapter 23

GIGI

Rex felt a mixture of emotions about Gigi, what she revealed in the meeting with Steve. At first, he felt blindsided, angry, and upset. Rex blamed her for not telling him. He had trusted her, confided in her. How could she have kept it secret?

But as she revealed why she did it, he started to understand. He knew she was remorseful.

After Steve left, Gigi had cried. All her pent-up emotions from her ordeal, the accident, the nightmares—everything resurfaced.

Hearing her sob broke his heart. Rex moved closer to her on the couch. He wrapped his arms around her, holding her tight. They rocked ever so slightly with each heave of her sobbing.

He held on, not letting Gigi go until her crying subsided and her tears ran dry.

Chapter 24
DR. KITE

HE WOKE UP, JUST LIKE that, without the rude awakening of an alarm. He had slept well. Refreshed, Kite stretched, feeling good. What was it about today? The thought of Tiffany brought on a slow smile. He applauded himself for being patient. Soon he would see her again, in the afternoon.

He busied himself around the apartment, straightening things up. Before noon, he stepped out to walk downtown to look for a new shirt to wear. It was slim pickings at the general store, but he managed to find something.

Keeping alive the hope that flickered, he could hardly wait.

Chapter 25

LILLY

LILLY PULLED UP ALONG THE street, looking for Tiffany's apartment. She glanced at Steve, sitting in the passenger seat, which was tilted back to accommodate his long legs. He looked comfortable, sprawled out like that. "We're almost there."

"We made good time."

It was still morning, early. On impulse, Lilly blurted, "I could do with some coffee now."

"Wouldn't hurt to get something to eat too," said Steve. "I don't know about you, but I'm hungry. We've got some time to spare."

Lilly was already turning down the street.

The only place in town was the Square Meal.

She pointed to a table in the back, leading the way as the waitress hurried to snatch a couple of menus and place settings.

"You folks new in town?" said the waitress.

Lilly glanced at her name tag. "Ruby, is it?"

Ruby nodded.

"Ruby, I'd like some coffee, scrambled eggs, and toast," said Lilly, handing the menu back.

Ruby scribbled on her pad, eager to take the orders.

"And you, sir?"

"Give me some of that bottomless cup of coffee," drawled Steve.

"You want yours black?"

"Any way you got, I'm easy. But if you'll bring me a creamer with some milk, I'd be doubly pleased," said Steve, grinning.

"Would you like some food to go with the coffee, sir?" said Ruby. If she were earning stars on her uniform, she'd be a five-star waitress for a five-star customer.

"Tell you what, just bring me today's special," said Steve.

"All righty," said Ruby, smiling.

Tiffany got up early. She didn't sleep well. After a restless night, she wasn't looking forward to the day. As if the stress of meeting with Kite wasn't enough, now Lilly was coming, driving from the city.

A long, hot shower was what she needed. She undressed, stepped into the tub, and turned on the water. She stood under the spray, closing her eyes, letting the water flow over her body. She stayed there, not moving, not reaching for the soap.

When she'd looked for an apartment, the shower was a

deal-breaker. She fell in love with another place, freshly painted mint green and cute as a button. A claw-foot tub sat in the middle of a small bathroom. In the end, however, she chose a simple apartment—cheap, clean, no frills, but with a shower.

There was something to be said about showers. They had a calming effect. Today was no different. Tiffany put on a pot of coffee, fried two eggs, toasted a couple of slices of bread, and smacked them together for an egg sandwich.

Chapter 26

LILLY

THE CAFFEINE DID THE WORK as adrenaline coursed through her veins, sending a jolt. Lilly's sleep had been cut short this morning, and the stress of sudden, last minute changes didn't sit well with her. Steve Cosine had merely said he was coming with her. He didn't ask or plead. He made the statement quietly, in a matter-of-fact manner. It almost didn't sink in when she heard it on the phone.

She knew it was pointless to argue with him. He was a man of quiet authority, who knew when and how to use it, and people respected him.

Sitting across the table from him at the diner, she studied Steve. He was sitting back in his chair, his shirt sleeves rolled up, looking relaxed. She thought, *Intelligent, but not cunning. A man of few words.* Tapping her finger, she smiled.

"Tired from driving?" said Steve.

"A bit, but I'm fine now."

"Good."

"I don't mean to pry," said Lilly, toying with her knife. "Why did you want to come?"

"To talk to Kite."

"Have you met him before?"

"No," said Steve.

"So it's your first time?"

Steve nodded.

"I almost didn't come," said Lilly.

"Why not?"

"I'm running a business, and we're down to the last two days of this session," said Lilly.

"What kind of session?"

"It's a program for women, two weeks of training and endurance."

Steve raised his brow. "How are you able to break away?'

"My assistant. She's a former top graduate, and she'll take care of it."

"You're leaving things in good hands?"

"Yeah, she's good." Lilly shifted in the seat, ready to get going. "Shall we?"

Steve picked up the tab on his way toward the cashier by the door.

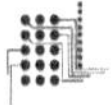

By the time they got to Tiffany's place, it was around noon.

Lilly knocked on the door and it swung open immediately.

"Tiffany," said Lilly, smiling in greeting.

Stepping forward, Tiffany gave her a quick hug as her

glance met Steve's.

"I'm Steve Cosine."

"A friend of Lilly?"

He didn't answer.

"He's here to talk to Kite," Lilly explained.

"Oh," said Tiffany, looking at first to Lilly then Steve.

"May we come in?" said Lilly. "We can talk about it."

Tiffany recapped and brought Steve up to date. She didn't see the point of holding anything back since Lilly had brought him here.

Lilly had heard most of this on the phone, but hearing all of it in person gave her more perspective. "So Kite is expecting your decision today on the two microchips?"

"Yes, and he'll be bringing them."

"Have you seen them?"

"He showed me the two injection pens, loaded with the chips," said Tiffany.

Steve cleared his throat. "How does Kite tell them apart?"

"The Number 9 pen has a dot on it," said Tiffany.

"A dot?"

"A black dot. I think he marked it with a magic marker."

"It's a little past one," said Lilly. "He should be here soon."

"Let me know if you have any other questions."

"I do," said Steve.

"Oh?" said Tiffany.

"What is your decision?"

Chapter 27
DR. KITE

HE ARRIVED AT TIFFANY'S DOOR at precisely half-past one. He straightened up, felt his clean-shaven cheeks, and sucked his breath in. Finally, he patted his pocket, feeling the reassuring outline of the two injection pens.

Ready at last, he knocked.

Tiffany opened the door, saying welcome as she attempted a smile, her nervousness betrayed by her fingers running through her hair.

Kite felt slightly awkward, sensing a bit of hesitancy in her. "Hello, is this a good time?"

"Oh yes, do come in," said Tiffany as she ushered him through the door.

His eyes pleaded with her for some show of warmth, before alighting on the two people standing farther back in the living room. He gulped. *It wasn't what he'd expected.*

"Let me introduce you all. Lilly Cooper and Steve Cosine."

His eyes traveled to the woman. Lilly, she looked familiar.

Then he remembered. She's the lady at Duggers—Lilly. One of the three women he had implanted mind-control chips.

Steve stepped forward; hand held out. "Steve Cosine."

He shook hands as he sought to find him in his memory banks. "I don't believe I've met you."

"You haven't," said Steve.

"So . . ."

"I'm here to ask you a few questions."

"About what?"

"For starters, your warehouse, Gary, the chips—"

Feeling his palms sweat, Kite started to panic. He thought, *You're busted. So busted.*

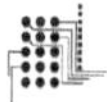

Tiffany spoke. "Kite came to my rescue the other day when I became dizzy at the store. He took me to the doctor and came by to check on me later."

Kite threw her a look of thanks.

She winked at him. At that moment, he relaxed a bit.

"I understand you have something to help her," said Steve.

"Well, yeah," said Kite, wondering how much he knew. What had she told him?

"She's told us," said Steve.

Kite threw a furtive glance at Tiffany.

"You have the chips," said Steve. "Did you bring them?"

A chill settled in his chest. *They know everything!*

Kite was silent. *Should he lie now? He could deny what he told Tiffany.*

He stole another look at Tiffany, noticed the thin line of her compressed lips. He thought, *If he lied, she would know. And he would be a liar to her.*

Kite nodded, resigned. "Yes," he whispered.

"Please bring them out," said Steve.

Kite reached in his pocket, carefully pulling out the two injection pens. He turned to Tiffany. "Have you decided?"

Tiffany was ready. "I'll try the medication tracker chip. I did get dizzy when I forgot my meds."

"Wait," said Lilly. "You're *sure* this is what you want?"

"I'm sure," said Tiffany, offering her arm to Kite.

Kite carefully checked for the mark, looking for the dot, before laying the Number 9 injection pen on the coffee table. He held the medication tracker pen. He nodded to Tiffany, pushing the clicker, preparing to inject the microchip.

Kite desperately wanted to inject the Number 9 chip in Tiffany. He paused, switching the pens, putting down the medication pen and picking up the Number 9 instead. "And this, have you given thought to it?" He approached Tiffany, extending an arm with the Number 9 pen in his hand.

Tiffany's fist slammed into Kite's chin, catching him by surprise, thrusting his head back.

Steve sprang into action, his hand grabbing Kite's wrist, trying to loosen his hold on the Number 9 pen.

They struggled as Kite cried out in alarm, gripping it more tightly. "Please, be careful."

Tiffany ducked under the swinging arms, trying not to get in the way.

"Grab it," yelled Lilly, shouting to her.

Tiffany watched the two men struggle, waiting for her opportunity to reach up and attempt to pull Kite's arm down.

Kite fought hard, as if all his life depended on it, refusing to give up the pen.

Steve exerted pressure, twisting Kite's arm.

Alarmed, Kite relaxed his grip on the injection pen as pain shot through his arm.

In a flash, Lilly snatched the Number 9 pen from his loosened grip.

Kite became outraged, pushing back on Steve, taking Tiffany with him. Tiffany rammed Kite's chest, using her head to push him hard.

Steve let go of him as Kite fell backward with Tiffany collapsing on top of him. They rolled on the floor before coming to a stop. Tiffany caught sight of the other pen that had been knocked off the coffee table onto the floor. She dropped her knee on Kite's chest and arched her back, extending her arm, reaching for the pen with the medication chip.

Across the room, Lilly pounced on Steve. She pushed up his sleeve as she aimed the injection pen on his bicep, clicking to inject the Number 9 chip. Lilly held on to him as skin touched skin, and Steve's pheromones mingled with hers. She kissed him on the lips, sealing his fate. *Their fate.*

Chapter 28
GIGI

She approached Rex's bed, eyes focused on his thin frame curled into a ball. The room was dark, the curtains drawn. She watched his chest rise and fall, listened to his raspy breathing, felt the faint pulse coursing through his vein, knew he was fighting for his life, each labored breath, each flutter of his heart refusing to give up. Sleep no longer provided solace from the pain. It hounded his body day by day, minute by minute. There was no escape. There was no quick end, no merciful death.

"Ah." An involuntary sound escaped her lips as Gigi stifled a cry, watching Rex. The man she loved lay there in bed, fighting for his life. Tears trickled down her cheeks as a wave of sadness overcame her. Gigi would not let him hear her cry. Rex deserved better than that. He hadn't asked for anything, hadn't complained. He was the shadow of a man now, what he used to be had long faded. She ached for the better days, days filled with brightness, laughter, and sunshine. Days where not a thought was given for darkness, for they were in love and on top of the world. They had everything to look forward to, a life together.

Gigi sighed, remembering that day at the cabin when he told her he was sick. She'd tried to suppress the sense of foreboding and fear and put on a brave front, shoving it to the back of her mind, determined to spend those precious few days together in their piece of heaven before coming back to the city, to the reality of life. They'd spoken not a word of his illness for the rest of the days there. Like a pact among friends and lovers, nothing remained to be said then, knowing there would be a time.

"Why?" she called out aloud, seeking an answer. What if she could have given up her foolish youth? If Gigi could have loved him earlier? If she could have more time with Rex? The silent room yielded no answers. She listened to his tortuous breathing, knew he was fighting for life, down to the very last breath. Rex would fight for her and their love.

"Please God, please," said Gigi, unable to hold back the flood of tears as she sank to the floor, sobbing, and for the first time in years begged for forgiveness, for help for someone other than herself, for someone she loved.

At that moment, as she got ready to surrender to the grief, she could feel his pain and the stubborn spark of life. Could she imagine her life without him? Rex, the person who stood by her through thick and thin. As she pleaded for Rex's life, the answer finally came to her.

Epilogue

SIX MONTHS LATER

Chapter 29

ELLEN

KNOCK, KNOCK.

"Mom and Dad, thanks for coming over this afternoon," said Ellen, opening her door.

"We picked up the balloons on our way here," said her dad, carrying a flotilla of Happy Birthday balloons.

Blowing a puckered kiss in the air, her mom bustled by with a white square box. "Wait until you see this cake! The bakers outdid themselves." She called out to her husband, "Honey, did you remember to bring the matches and the big candle with the number one?"

He winked at Ellen. "Yes, Grandma."

"Hey, you're no spring chicken either. *Grandpa.*"

"Where's Angie?" said Mrs. Fulbright, after she'd unloaded all her stuff.

"She's in her room, getting her diaper changed."

"Brad's here?"

"Yes, he's helping out."

"Nice," said her mom, eyeing the festive party room.

"You did the decorations?"

"I did, with Brad."

"So, how's your new job with the properties sales group?"

"Mom, it's not new anymore. Since I started three and a half months ago, I've sold four units," said Ellen.

"And you have more flexibility in your hours, right?"

"Yes, since I'm a commissioned salesperson. I work from nine to six every day, but my hours are flexible."

"I thought they offered you a staff position?"

"Yeah, if I wanted to be the salesperson for the condo. But I'd have to live in the building until it's all sold."

"You didn't want to move?"

"Nope. I like it here where I'm closer to you and Brad."

"I'm glad you are, dear."

"Yes, it's working out great, Mom," said Ellen. "I show the four different model condos that are available for people to see. It's nice."

"I'm glad. I was getting worried the way your old job was going—you know, with Andy."

Eager to change the subject, Ellen nodded approvingly at her mom's new outfit. "I like what you're wearing—a cute floral dress."

Her mom smiled, touching her arm. "And you look lovely, dear."

She turned to look at Brad as he came out of the bedroom, carrying a freshly diapered Angie. She asked him, "Your parents are coming?"

"This could be them now," said Brad, as another knock sounded.

Ellen rushed to the door and waited for Brad and Angie to catch up before opening it.

"Well hello," said Brad's mom, standing next to his dad, a large gift bag in her hands.

"Hi Mom, Dad," said Brad, leaning forward to greet them.

After a round of hugs, a clamor rose among the grandparents fighting to hold Angie. Ellen smiled as she retreated to the kitchen. Brad quickly followed to get the dishes for the table.

"Let's leave the smash cake in the kitchen until it's time," said Ellen. "You've got your camera?"

"I've got it here," said Brad, smiling as he carefully set it next to the smash cake. "You got a good one, a frosted white cake decorated with a penguin, Angie's favorite stuffed toy."

"Uh, Brad?"

"What?"

"I'm glad you're here."

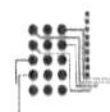

The party was a success. Angie, smashing the cake with both hands and scooping the penguin—captured on video, in all its glory. They watched the replay, howling with laughter. Angie's first birthday was a hoot.

They sat around chatting for awhile, filled with good food. Ellen finally stood up, bringing the dirty dishes into the kitchen.

Ellen's mom came up behind her. "Let me help you with that."

"No, that's okay, Mom. You go out there and relax," said Ellen. "I'm going to wash and Brad'll dry the dishes."

"How about we take Angie to the park for a few hours, enjoy the day and walk off the calories?"

"Brad's parents?"

"We'll take them. It'll be a lovely walk in the park, especially this time of the day."

"Thanks, Mom," said Ellen.

Fifteen minutes later, she stuck her head back in the kitchen. "I've got Angie's diapers, bottles, and all her stuff. You guys want to meet us grandparents for a birthday dinner? Give you a break from the cooking."

Ellen glanced at Brad.

"Where and when, Mom?" asked Ellen.

"How about the one you guys like so much, you know, with the deep blue sea like stepping into Neptune's world?"

Brad laughed as Ellen squealed with delight.

As the front door shut, she handed a towel to Brad. "Ready to work?"

He rolled up his sleeves. Dipping his hands in the soapy water of the sink, Brad scooped a handful of suds and dabbed it on her nose and cheeks. "Now you look funny."

"Hey, quit that," she said, laughing. "Not fair."

He grabbed his camera and took a picture. Grinning, he said, "I'm holding this for ransom. You'd better be a good girl."

"Oh no, you don't," said Ellen as she tried to catch his arm.

Slipping easily out of her grasp, he laid the camera down in a safe spot.

She was ready for him when he came back, flicking suds on his head.

Brad bent over with laughter as bubbles slid down his hair and wet his shirt. He reached for the hose spray and pointed it straight at her.

She shrieked. "Don't you dare!"

"Watch me," he yelled as he directed a spray of water at her.

She shook her hand, flinging water on the floor as she rushed to wrestle the spray from him.

He was too quick for her and sprayed another one before she could get to him.

They fought over the hand-held sprayer, spraying water on each other.

Finally, out of breath, she was the first to hold her hand up. "Truce."

"You give up?"

"No, we give up at the same time. That's what a truce is."

Brad laughed. "Okay, on the count of three. One, two, three." He put the spray hose back in its slot on the kitchen sink.

"Look at us," said Ellen as water dripped from her head and soaked her top. Looking down, she realized that the wet cotton material was clinging to her breasts, her nipples standing erect.

Brad's eyes followed, staring.

They stood, frozen for a millisecond before bursting out in laughter. Brad held out his arms, pulling her close as he leaned down to kiss her.

She took a step back until she felt the edge of the sink digging in her back.

He moved with her, his lips clinging to hers, not letting go.

She responded to him, the soft probing of his tongue, while the odd sensation of his wet jeans, rough against her bare, smooth legs, filtered through her mind.

They stood there, arms wrapped around each other, and kissed.

When Ellen finally came up for air, she met his eyes and saw the warmth tinged with desire and tenderness. With love.

She glanced at the clock. "We have two hours before dinner . . ."

He laughed. "That's enough time for me to finish *two* desserts."

She led the way down the hall to the bedroom, stopping to grab dry towels from the hall closet.

He patted her with the towel, taking the time to dab her face and hair, then he slowly peeled off her wet shirt and unsnapped her bra before unzipping her skirt. Brad took off his soggy shirt and pants, then lifted Ellen, carrying her to the bed. Unhurried, he dried her from head to toe with slow, tender movements. When he finished, he lay down beside her and let her dry him off.

He watched as she worked, enjoying every minute of it.

She made no effort to hide her body—the telltale signs of weight loss on her flesh, the loose skin, and the striped marks of pregnancy in plain sight.

He saw her, exposed to him, in the light. "You're beautiful, just the way you are."

She caressed his face, tracing her fingers along the muscular contours of his arm. She buried her face in the soft curls of his hairy chest. "I missed you, Brad."

"I've missed you too." He tilted her chin up with his finger and kissed her, surrendering to the softness of her lips.

She murmured, eyes closed, entranced with this moment, one that she had so longed for, one she wanted never to let go. "Can you just hold me, Brad?"

Brad wrapped his arms around her, feeling her quiver as he held her. He pulled his head back to look at her face, into her eyes, and saw the tears. He gently kissed her face and the wetness on her cheeks. "I'm here, Ellen," he said. "I love you."

"I love you," she whispered back.

He kissed her again, tasting the salt of her tears. "Baby, I'm here to stay."

Chapter 30

LILLY

THE TWELVE WOMEN SAT IN a circle, fresh-faced and excited, meeting each other for the first time on day one of the program. Naomi and Tiffany had signed them in, ushered them to the chairs.

A floor-to-ceiling window covered an entire wall of the new warehouse, rebuilt on the grounds of an old one that had been burnt down in a storm—on top of Kite's old warehouse. The sunlight streamed in the room lit only by natural light at this time of the day. The decor was modern and clean-lined. A white leather couch placed along one wall. A vase of cut flowers, its colors vibrant, fresh, welcoming, graced a small whitewashed birch table near the entry.

The door opened. Heads turned.

In strode an elegant woman dressed in a tailored suit. Beside her, an older man with a smooth, relaxed stride, a full head and shoulders taller than her, his weathered face ruggedly handsome,

The air bristled with something akin to sparks. Two people so different, individuals comfortable in their own right, standing together. One tall, one short. One wearing a casual jacket with a cotton shirt and a slightly crooked tie, one well-dressed. A man and a woman, facing them together.

"Ladies, welcome to our program. My name is Lilly Cooper." She turned to the man, touching his hand. "This is my husband, Steve Cosine."

They stood together as if they were one. Steve's eyes on her. Puppy love eyes.

Magnetism emitted from the couple. More refined than animal attraction. Twelve pairs of eyes feasted on them, unable to tear away—power, charm, something they couldn't put their hands on, fascinated them.

Steve joined hands with her, fingers intertwined.

Lilly smiled. *This time it feels right. All of it.*

Chapter 31
GIGI

THE HAIRDRESSER TUCKED ONE MORE strand into Gigi's fancy coiffure. A work of art the hairdresser took all morning to build. Pleased with the result, she stepped back. Passing the hand-held mirror to Gigi, she swiveled her chair, turning her around until her back was facing the large wall mirror. "Here, have a look."

"Thanks," said Gigi. Holding the mirror, she spun in her chair, viewing her profile, turning to see the back of her hair. She caught sight of her face, seeing the newly etched lines around her eyes, forehead, and mouth. No longer fighting it, but accepting of it. Not only that, the tinnitus had returned, but she'd learn to live with it with the help of supplemental therapies and new treatments. Snatching the tube of pink watermelon lipstick, she touched up her lips, nodding to the hairdresser, ready for the bridal veil. She smiled. *A girl's gotta look good on her special day!*

Walking down the aisle, hearing the sounds of music drifting closer, Gigi focused on Rex, standing there and waiting to start the rest of their lives together. Rex—the love of her life. She quickly blinked a few times, overcome with emotion.

Rex stood tall and straight, sporting a healthy tan and glow, muscles filling out his shirt, full of new energy, his illness cured, his body healed.

His brown eyes locked on her as a smile lit up his face, the boyish grin Gigi knew so well. She saw the love in his eyes spilling out in abundance. Reaching Rex at the altar, she touched him knowingly on his arm, the spot of his implanted microchip—the one extracted from Gigi's arm.

Chapter 32
DR. KITE

PEOPLE TRICKLED IN AS THE word got out, going to the check stations to find out if they had the microchip implants. It was hard to tell how many had been innocent victims because the warehouse fire destroyed the records. But, starting from a few every night in the beginning, the numbers had increased over a period of a couple of years. So it was possible that a few thousand people may have become unwitting subjects. For the "lucky" ones who had it, it became a prized possession.

Gigi had been the first one to go through this procedure with Rex. It had been simple enough. It took less than the four minutes touted for cataract surgery.

She had come up with the idea and proposed it. Gigi somehow became the poster child—her face and name synonymous with this campaign. A unique opportunity for people willing to donate their microchip. On their applications, they could indicate names of family members or friends who needed the chip. If the name of the recipient was left blank, strangers were matched in the process after an extensive algorithm provided paired names, and face-to-face meetings firmed the decisions. People had to apply and undergo an assessment to ensure no coercion was behind it. The only requirement; it had to be a willing act of unselfishness.

They came out with it in a big way with public announcements on TV, radio, billboard ads, and social media. Gigi became a media darling, synonymous with "Saving Rex," which grew into "Saving Someone."

They filmed the process each step of the way in a documentary. Rex and his illness. Gigi and hers. The filmmakers made sure to include the part about the mind-control chips but stressed that no one had those implanted chips anymore. Kite did not appear in the film except for one clip showing him in prison garb. A brief mention accompanied the clip—Kite had become born-again, and he would be eligible for parole in five years.

The response to the "Saving Someone" campaign turned out better than Gigi had anticipated. Initially, angry outbursts and debates crowded the airwaves. Supporters and detractors had their say. It generated a rowdy response.

Gigi watched the long line of people forming with those arriving well before the early morning opening. There was joviality in the air, laughter sprinkled here and there, a mood of hope and anticipation of what awaited at the end of the line.

Funding from legitimate sources furthered research into Kite's mind-control microchips, yielding some surprising preliminary results. He finally came clean with Gigi, Ellen, and Lilly. When the men brought Gigi to the warehouse after her car accident, Kite had removed the first defective mind-control chip from Gigi's arm. He stored that microchip in the warehouse, but unfortunately the fire destroyed it.

Kite ultimately removed the other two mind-control chips from Ellen and Lilly before serving his prison sentence. Tests on these two chips finally revealed which of the two was the defective microchip—the one he retrieved from Lilly.

Deep within the recesses of the human brain, the battle between the chip and the unconscious mind had raged. It had come down to this. But the tipping point, what Kite did not foresee, was the one thing the mind-control chip could not overcome—the *primal will* to survive.

THE END of the Alterations Trilogy

www.ingramcontent.com/pod-product-compliance
Lightning Source LLC
Chambersburg PA
CBHW051608100726
47898CB00001B/282